Journey THROUGH A *Rainbow*

Francis Eugene Wood

A book for Mihomi
all my best to you.

Francis E. Wood '19

Tip of the Moon Publishing Co.

Published by Tip-of-the-Moon Publishing Company
Farmville, Virginia

Book design by Jon Marken
Photograph of author by Chris Wood
Cover art and illustrations by Martha Pennington Louis
Printed by Farmville Printing Company

First USA Printing

E-mail address: fewwords@moonstar.com
Website: www.tipofthemoon.com
Or write to: Tip-of-the-Moon Publishing Company
175 Crescent Road, Farmville, Virginia 23901

ISBN: 978-0-9829121-0-2

Acknowledgments

"I wrote another book. Now let's fix it." I have made this statement often to my wife over the years. And she has obliged to help me render it readable for the book lovers. But there are others who have also been there for me whenever I dream on paper. They proof my work, tidying my sentence structure, punctuation, and spelling. All the things I don't have time for in the process of recording the scenes in my head. My thanks to my aunt, Jeanne Clabough, Tina Dean, and Jon Marken, who have all offered their time and expertise in bringing my stories to the bookshelf. Laurie Jensen joins the fold of accomplished editors on this publication, adding her substantial skills to the final manuscript. Welcome aboard, Laurie. Thanks to Jon Marken for being the best at what he does. And to my wife, Chris, for her interest in my thoughts and her dedication to my work. Finally, thanks to all of you book lovers, who encourage me to continue dreaming on paper.

F.E.W.

Author's Note

I have had this title for many years but just sat down to write it on the sixth day of January, 2013. A dozen sittings later, it was finished. The story line went through several incarnations in my mind over the years until one morning I woke up with the one you are about to read. As with most of my stories, this one grew from people and experiences I have known, along with a lifetime fascination with rainbows. As a boy, I often imagined what it would be like to enter a rainbow. I did not merely desire to be over one, like Dorothy in *The Wizard of Oz*, but instead, within its realm of colors, like seas in my mind. Mystical seas, where currents of wisdom moved me from one level of enlightenment to the next, until finally I would realize the answers to questions life posed to me. And adventures? Of course, I imagined adventures in the realm of a rainbow. Who wouldn't? The fact that the main character of this story, Theodore Clatterbuck, is dreadfully bullied at school (and away from it) is based on a truth I will not divulge. Even his dog, Martha, a chocolate Lab I know by a different name, is so real I can see her now. And Captain Roy G. Biv...well, I could go on and on, but I'll stop here and allow you to turn the pages and enter into a place you can hardly imagine, if it were not for the fact that someone has been there and back again.

Dedication

This story is dedicated
to the joy one feels while
witnessing the gift of
a rainbow.

Clouds gathered in the eastern sky as the boy dragged the point of a long, thin stick through the gritty, loose dirt and sand that bordered the broken pavement of the narrow road. A single-lane iron bridge stood in the distance, shaded by towering hardwood trees that dressed the steep slope on the opposite side of the river.

"Martha," Theodore Clatterbuck said softly as he looked past the entrance of the bridge to the other side, where waited his best friend. Theodore smiled and quickened his pace.

As the boy approached, the chocolate Lab barked and anxiously sniffed the air while fighting her inclination to run to him.

Theodore stepped onto the bridge and tossed the stick out over the iron rails. He bent forward and slapped his legs above the patches on his knees. "Come on, girl!" he called.

Martha bolted like a Belmont thoroughbred, and in seconds was lapping at the face and neck of her favorite human.

"That's my girl," Theodore said as he reached into his shirt pocket for a leftover morsel of the sandwich his mother had made for him that morning for his school lunch. "Here you go." He offered the now stale chunk of bread with a sliver of ham. The boy laughed aloud as the Lab inhaled the offering. "You didn't even taste it, did you, girl?" Theodore rubbed Martha's head and cupped her satiny ears in his hands. "You been waiting long?" he asked as he stood up and looked over the bridge rail. The river was low. Theodore stared down into a sun-streaked eddy where sunfish flashed their glittering gills while darting back and forth in mock competition.

Martha waited patiently at the boy's side for the next overture of attention toward her. A rumble in the distance broke Theodore's trance, and he walked along, slapping the bridge rails with one hand and teasing Martha with the other. "It might rain, Martha." Theodore looked up past the iron bridge beams as he spoke. The sky was still clear above him. "Or maybe not here," he continued. "Let's race to the house." Theodore ran only a few feet before Martha went past him. The scent of honeysuckle wafted in the warm breeze as boy and dog left the bridge with Theodore trailing a pitiful second behind Martha.

Bea Clatterbuck was standing on the back porch of the small wood-framed house nestled beneath giant oaks and flowering magnolia trees when a long roll of thunder gained her attention. She finished shucking the ears of corn she was tending to for supper and looked out across the rolling hills at the sky. "I sure hope you are coming this way for a change," she said quietly to herself. The woman shifted her gaze to the edge of the yard where a small and ragged garden struggled in dried dirt. She shook her head and cut the rotten end off an ear of corn. "Wormy," she said in disgust. The woman was about to turn back into the house when Martha came running around the corner. Bea smiled upon seeing the dog. "Well, look at you, girl. You left him in the dust again." Moments later, Theodore appeared and made an elaborate hoax of falling at his mother's feet with breathless pleas for sustenance, all the while fending off repeated mock attacks by Martha.

Bea stood for a moment and watched her son's antics and then turned toward the back door. "There's a spoonful or two of apple crisp in the fridge and some tea in the pitcher." She grasped the screen door handle and looked back at her son. "How was school today?" she asked.

Theodore sat up and spanked the dead grass from the knees of his pants. "Oh, Mama, it was so good that I just can't wait until it ends."

"Well, you best be getting those tests studied for, because next week comes the finals."

Theodore smiled at his mother and her mild scold,

but was not disrespectful in his response. "Making the grade is easy enough, Mama." He followed the woman into the house. Martha passed him in the doorway. "It's mostly the rest of it that makes it a chore." The boy moved across the small kitchen and opened the refrigerator, where he took out a saucer-sized plate covered with aluminum foil. He grasped the tea pitcher with the other hand and closed the refrigerator door with his knee. He then walked over to the kitchen table and sat down.

As Theodore was unwrapping his plate, Bea placed a fork and a glass beside it. Then she walked to the sink and began washing the ears of corn. "You still having trouble with those boys?" she asked without looking at her son. "Is that one named Bently Card still taunting you?"

Theodore finished his apple crisp in three scoops and drank half of his glass of tea before answering. "Bently Card," he repeated the name. "That boy's got everybody thinking I'm just a poor hick that's good for nothing."

Bea Clatterbuck heard a sudden anguish in her son's voice and turned toward him. "Well now, don't you fret over him at all, son. Anything he says will reflect back on him one day."

"Yeah," the boy answered. "So you say." He got up from the table and was out of the kitchen before his mother could respond.

Martha sensed the boy's mood and sat watching him as he walked away.

Bea shook her head as she noticed the puzzled look

in the Lab's eyes. "Well, go on with him," she pointed at the kitchen door. "He'll talk more to you than he will to me."

Theodore sat on the picnic table on the back porch and looked at the sky to the east. He could smell the rain, but the wind was carrying the dark clouds farther to the south. The afternoon sunlight was beginning to send tree shadows into the field when suddenly the boy became aware of a most breathtaking sight. "Mama!" he called. "Come out here—quick!"

Bea pushed open the door thinking the boy had hurt himself, when she saw the reason for his excitement. Slowly she walked over to where he sat and stood beside him. "Well, I'll swannee," she lamented with wide eyes. "I've never seen one so vivid as that."

"You can see all the colors so well." Theodore was amazed. He had seen rainbows before, had even studied them in school, but never had he witnessed such a spectacular display as this. "It's like God has painted the sky, Mama."

Bea's amazement rendered her momentarily speechless, but she nodded in agreement with her son.

"Just think, Mama," the boy spoke in wonderment, "just imagine, if you could walk right up on it and escape this world, up there where everything has got to be beautiful. God wouldn't allow meanness there, would He?"

Bea heard the words of her son and understood why he would speak that way. A sickly child, Theodore had no siblings and had parents who were far past the ages of those of his peers. His father, Virgil, a farmhand, was a good man but lacked the talent and ability to lift his family out of the poverty they had suffered together. A place to call his own would never be. Instead, he rented wherever he moved his wife and son. No place was home for long for the Clatterbucks. Possessions were few, friends scarce. There was hardly time for developing friendships before Virgil would tire of his current job and decide to move on. Bea's love for the man outweighed her displeasure with their nomadic lifestyle, and long before their son was born, she had resigned herself to a life on the move. Seldom were the Clatterbucks in one place for more than a year or two. They never joined a church or became involved with a community. Bea felt it was too late for her and her husband, but she wanted more for their son. She wanted Theodore to have a home, a base. A place he could call his own. She spoke of her concern for the boy's future with her husband, but the man could not realize a life he had never had. "We've got to move with the crops," he would tell her. The owners of the farms he worked up and down the east coast expected him to hire on with them each year. He would manage everything from corn to peanuts and tobacco to cotton, just like his father and grandfather before him. Farming and growing things for others was all Virgil Clatterbuck knew. If he ever wanted anything else for himself or his wife and son, he never spoke of it. But there were times that Bea saw a hesitation in the man. Brief moments of hope leapt into her heart when he was slow to answer her concerns about Theodore. "He ain't cut like me," Virgil once told her. "His bones are thin, and his back ain't strong." Seldom would the man mention the boy's weak heart, which a doctor had diagnosed when Theodore was six years old. That diagnosis had frightened Bea to the point where she became very protective of him. He was never allowed to work at strenuous chores. His daily race with Martha up the road from the bridge worried the woman more than she would admit. But she allowed it with reservations. "There's no way you can outrun that dog," she would remind him. "So don't try too hard."

The boy liked adventures, so she seldom stopped him from wandering off as long as he was back home by specific times. She encouraged him to share his adventures with other boys, but that had always been difficult. Usually the boys in school avoided him. Physically he was awkward, with long, thin limbs and hips that seemed out of sync. His feet were long and narrow, and he had a lumbering gait. Theodore possessed no athletic ability at all, so ball games were disastrous affairs for him on the school playground. The teasing and abuse from the boys were hurtful memories for him that piled on from year to year. Theodore avoided most interaction with his classmates when at all possible, which set him even more apart. Academically he was very sharp, which usually endeared him to his teachers who often showed him favoritism in class, and that would later lead to more teasing by jealous classmates and even bullying by some of the more maladjusted boys. There were afternoons when Theodore would come home with a bruised shoulder or shin from unearned punishment inflicted upon him by a jealous hand or foot. The boy was an expert at hiding his wounds from his parents, unless a fist or stone cut or bruised his cheek. Once, his mother discovered a long, angry whelp across his back and jagged puncture marks above his kidneys. It was only after much questioning that she learned from her son that this punishment was dealt him because out of twenty-six boys and girls, he alone achieved an A+ on a math test. It was against Theodore's pleas that Bea addressed the incident with the school superintendent, Mr. Bellendork, who promised the abuse would not go unpunished. And, indeed, the man was true to his word, even if the father of Bently Card did, in a drunken rage, go off on the principal during a twenty minute phone tirade in which he threatened to have the academic veteran fired from his position and ruined in the community. Mr. Card had also visited David Horton, Virgil Clatterbuck's employer, and spun his liquored-up version of the incident to his long-time golfing buddy. Horton, who knew better than most his friend's temperament and the foul nature of his son, advised Virgil not to escalate the situation by allowing his wife to pursue it any further.

The Clatterbucks were advised to go out of their way both at school and in the community to avoid the Cards. It was an ineffective remedy to a festering sore, as a slight admonishment to Bently Card was like the annoyance of a gnat bite on the neck. He merely ceased using sticks and stones to persecute Theodore and instead, wrought vindictiveness against the boy in front of his schoolmates whenever the opportunity presented itself. And the bully thought himself clever, as he was sly not to spew his cruel and hurtful abuses at the boy within earshot of an adult. Some classmates snickered or laughed out of fear for themselves. No one wanted to be singled out and ostracized by Bently for not going along with his antics. Others stayed their distance in an effort to avoid the guilt they felt for not intervening in a situation they knew was wrong.

There was one individual, however, who did not fear Bently Card. Her name was Becky Bloom. A bright and articulate girl, she was not at all reluctant to intercede on Theodore's behalf whenever she was present at one of Bently's attacks on him. "You are a wicked sort," she would scold the bad-tempered boy. "One day you are going to have to see yourself the way everyone else does," she told him once to his face. "That will either be the end of you or the beginning of who you can be."

The meaning of the girl's words were far beyond Bently's comprehension. He responded with a scowl and a warning to mind her own business, or she "might get what Clatterbuck was gonna get."

It was obvious to everyone that Becky Bloom did not cower to Bently Card's threats. She was the only daughter of Mayor Bob Bloom and his wife, Nancy. She knew the Cards and had dealt with Bently since kindergarten. "He's got issues you don't even want to hear about," she told Theodore one day as the two class-mates walked from the school bus to Becky's driveway, a short distance from the iron bridge. "But you've got to stand up to him, Theo, or he will continue to make your life miserable."

Becky was really Theodore's only friend. She would often ride her bike over to his house across the river. They studied together, and sometimes she would accompany him on an adventure. Theodore had liked the girl since his family had moved into the gatehouse at the Horton farm two years prior. But now, he liked her even more. They were both fourteen years old, and the boy was not about to ruin their friendship with a youthful revelation. His instincts told him that she really liked him, too, although there was no rush to talk about it.

The truth was Becky liked most everything about Theodore Clatterbuck. He was smart and unique. And he had a very handsome face. His jaw was a little weak, but his smile was bright and cheerful. His eyes were the bluest she had ever seen. They sparkled whenever he told her a story. His hair was blonde and usually needed a trim, but he was not averse to her touching it up a bit around his ears and neck with his mother's scissors.

Bea Clatterbuck welcomed Becky into their home, although she guessed the mayor and his wife would have preferred another friend other than her son for their daughter's affections. The truth was that Bea saw in Becky hope for her son. The girl always seemed to be in tune with his nature. Becky could reach him when it was at times difficult for his own mother to understand him.

"Bently Card is extremely envious of Theo, Miz

Bea," the girl once told her. "He's a lonely, spoiled boy who has never had the affection of his parents. Every mean thing he says or does is a cry for their attention."

Bea understood what Becky was telling her. She appreciated the girl's wish to make her understand the nature of her son's nemesis.

"Bently will continue to push him as long as Theo allows it," Becky said one day as Theodore sat at the picnic table sketching with pencil and pad the magnolia tree that stood at the corner of the yard.

"But he can't fight him. He hasn't got the strength or ability." Bea stood beside the girl and watched her son drawing.

Becky smiled. "Don't you worry, Miz Bea. One day Theo will know how to handle Bently Card. I know he will."

Bea smiled at the faith Becky had in her son.

Virgil Clatterbuck knocked lightly on his son's bedroom door and turned the doorknob with calloused fingers.

"Come in." Theodore laid the open book in his lap and leaned back against the headboard of his bed.

Virgil opened the door and stepped into the room. "Studying a little late tonight?" The man shuffled across the room as he spoke.

Theodore could smell the sweat of the day's work on his father's clothes. "Yes, sir. I've got a pretty big science test tomorrow."

Virgil stood at the bedside, his hands in his pockets. He looked at the open book. "Stars and the solar system, planets." He paused. "You know it all?"

Theodore joined the fingers of both hands behind the nape of his neck. "I've got it down pretty well. I think I'll do all right."

His father nodded his head. "Everything okay at school?" Virgil scratched the back of his head and looked up at the ceiling. "I mean, is that Card boy giving you trouble?"

Theodore shook his head. "No, sir," he lied. "No trouble."

Virgil knew better. "You know, son, I been thinkin' it's time for us to move on. I mean after the crops are in, maybe head on down to Florida for a spell. You'd like it down there. We ain't been that far south since you was a tot, and I know you don't remember it none. What do you think?"

Theodore knew what his father was doing. He had done it before. Offer up the possibility of a better life and then let it go. It was a habit born of guilt. There would be no move to Florida. The best the family had ever done was in Virginia. There was no need to change, unless a new outlook on life came with it. But sadly, his father's dreams were never vivid, his focus never clear, and his self-confidence was cluttered with regrets. A good but simple man, he was marked from the beginning for a non-descriptive passage through this world.

Theodore loved his father but had never really spoken freely with him. "It's okay here, dad," the boy answered. "There's a thousand Bently Cards out there. The next would be waiting in Florida."

Virgil nodded his head. "Yeah," he responded quietly. "I guess you're right. I just don't know what to do to end it."

Theodore picked up his book and changed the subject. "Did you see that rainbow today? I'd never seen the colors so distinct before. That was the widest arch I've ever seen."

The man smiled at his son. "Yeah, I saw it. Smelled the rain, too. Hoped it would come this way." He turned to leave the room and then stopped and looked out the window into the darkness. "You know, my dad once told me that everything you need to know in life can be found in the colors of the rainbow." Virgil tilted his head as if he was prying an old thought. "It was something about the colors that he said people are drawn to. They mean something, but I'm not clear-headed enough to remember." The man shook his head in defeat. "Goodnight, Son." Virgil walked out of the bedroom and closed the door behind him.

Theodore turned to a chapter in his textbook that dealt with rainbows. He read it all and then closed the book and turned out his light. For several minutes, he imagined himself balancing on a rainbow. His feet were splashing in hues of orange and red as he slipped between the colors and fell upon a cloud, weightless and drifting.

"Almost five years," Virgil said to his wife as he sat on the edge of their bed. "We've been here almost five years and don't have much to show for it."

Bea put her book down in her lap and took off her reading glasses, laying them on the bedside table. She looked at her husband, his slumped shoulders and bowed head. Gently, she touched his back and said, "This is a good place, Virgil, and Mr. Horton is pleased with your work. He told me last week that you are the best farm manager he's ever had. The crops produced, and you've done well for him at the cattle market."

Virgil raked his hair slowly with his fingers. "Yeah, I've put some money in Mr. Horton's bank account, but not much in ours." He turned to his wife. "I feel like I'm spinnin' my wheels in the mud, Bea."

Bea could see the anguish on her husband's face. A furrow in his brow and the shadow of the lamplight made distinguishable the long wrinkles across his forehead. He looked older to her. Older since the last time she noticed.

"I did want more for you and Theo by now. I wanted a home of our own and a plot of land in our name, somethin' to leave you and the boy." Virgil clenched the bed sheet with his fist. "If we move south in the fall, it'll just be the same as always. Workin' for the man. Scratchin' out a meager livin', gettin' nowhere." He rubbed his chin with the palm of his hand. "I pray to get ahead, Bea. I watch you workin' and puttin' in a garden every year and cannin' and all, and I just want somethin' more for you, that's all. Just somethin' more.

And Theo." The man shook his head slowly and looked at the photo of the boy and his mother on the chest of drawers. "He's such a good and bright kid. And I got no time for him. I got no dreams to give him. Just a hope and a prayer that he'll find his way in this world." Virgil stopped and touched his wife's hand. "I worry about him all the time. His weak heart and what the doctor said about that, and his hips as he gets older." The man tightened his jaw and looked down at the floor before he continued. "And then, them boys at school. The bad ones, who've teased and taunted him because he isn't like them. Bently Card. He's the worst of the lot. For all we know, we got no real sense of what Theo has gone through all his life. He'll never say it all. Not Theo. He deals with the bullyin' his own way, coverin' up the bruises and shyin' away from the truth of it. But what gets me the worst is what it does to him inside. What can he really think about this world? What can he really think about me for not steppin' in and stoppin' it? Horton tells me to ignore it and not to confront Bill Card about his son, or the man could make it bad for us. But I'm thinkin' I've got nothin' to lose but this job."

Bea squeezed her husband's hand. "You got the world weighing you down, Virgil," she spoke softly, carefully. "You'll do what's right. I've been praying on it for a long time. The Lord will look out for us. I have no doubt of it. In His way, He will grant us all what we need. He already did it when He gave me you and Theo. I wouldn't ask for more for myself. But for our son, I do pray that a dream will come true."

Virgil lay down beside his wife as she turned out the light. "You're a good woman, Bea Clatterbuck. The good Lord did bless me with you and then, for some reason, gave me a fine son to raise. Maybe if we pray hard enough, a dream might come true for him." Virgil was tired. He closed his eyes and felt his wife snuggle next to him.

"And maybe, one for you," Bea whispered. "I'll pray for that, too."

THE LAST WEEK OF SCHOOL PASSED at a snail's pace for Theodore. But each day brought him closer to the world he found solace in. A world separated from the pressures that laced his life like ragged shoestrings. Each morning when he walked across the iron bridge, he felt it. A weight that bore down on him, suppressing the core of his nature and rendering him quiet and aloof. His true nature became locked deep inside, hidden from all but one. Becky Bloom was the last person to see the boy each day before he disappeared into the protective shell that set him apart from his classmates. Even his teachers only knew him as a bright academic student, shaded in mystery. Never would he volunteer a fact about his life outside of school, and yet, in his quiet and shy demeanor, his teachers perceived a level of wisdom seldom found in children his age. The fact that the awkward boy was teased was known by most of his teachers, and it was not tolerated in their presence, for there was a tendency on their part to be protective of him. And it was not a secret that Becky Bloom, the mayor's daughter, was not only fond of him, but would stand up for him at any cost. When the girl witnessed a teacher allowing even the slightest degree of abuse toward Theodore from the likes of Bently Card or his sort, she would ignite a public tirade that even the more seasoned teacher would rather avoid. Becky Bloom was not a typical fourteen-year-old student. She was, in fact, at the top of her class in academics, a bold and strong-willed girl, who would just as soon confront a sour-natured teacher as she would a student who fell upon her distastes for anything she construed as wrong or unfair. She was a force to contend with. Well-liked by most and avoided by some, she seemed unconcerned with the more shallow attitudes. She was smart and serious and quite pretty to the young males' eyes. But she was not for that. Her lighter side was seen only by a few close friends. And there was only one friend whose trust she shared in a way that allowed her guarded inner self to emerge whenever she was with him.

Becky bent down and rubbed Martha vigorously behind the ears. "How's the sweetest dog I know doing this morning?" she asked as Theodore joined her at the mouth of her driveway.

The morning sun was shining on Martha's satiny ears as she reveled in the girl's attention. "It's the last day you'll have to watch Theo leave you for a whole summer's vacation!" Excitement was in the girl's voice.

Martha lapped at Becky's chin. When the girl stood up, the dog turned to Theodore for what she knew would be his final pat on her head and command to return to the other side of the iron bridge. The boy spiced the ritual with a treat from his pocket.

"How old is Martha now?" Becky asked while watching the chocolate Lab retreat to the bridge.

"I got her just before we came here to live. She was about four months old." Theodore turned around and saw the dog cross to the other side of the river. Then he turned and continued to walk up to the fork of the road, where the school bus would arrive in ten minutes.

"Are you ready for that science final today?" Becky asked.

"Yeah, I guess so." There was no animation in the boy's answer.

The girl looked over at her friend. "Listen, Clatterbuck," she scolded playfully, "don't be clamming up on me today. I had an earful from Mom this morning about being a sweet little girl and not correcting my teachers, which is a direct response to a call last night from Mr. Lynn about that little incident in class the other day when I informed him that his zipper was down, and the faded Les Paul guitar on his boxers was definitely vintage."

Theodore smiled and looked at the girl. "I heard about that. And when did you become an expert on vintage guitars?"

"My dad has one just like the one the whole class saw on Mr. Lynn's boxers."

Theodore chuckled. "Your dad played the guitar?" he asked as if surprised.

"Yes, he did. And quite well, too. Just ask him sometime."

"Did he play in a band?" Theodore was always interested in the things Becky would bring up.

"Yes, but it was really dumb. I mean, they called themselves The Electric Figs."

The boy laughed. "You mean, like in Fig Newtons?"

Becky rolled her eyes. "Maybe I shouldn't have told you about that. Anyway, they didn't go anywhere with it. Just played for parties and a few school dances."

Theodore smiled at the thought of Mr. Bloom, the town mayor, with an electric guitar balancing on his robust belly and his shining bald head reflecting the glare of spotlights. Of course, the idea that the man was ever young and cool could hardly be imagined by the boy.

The bus came around the bend in the road just as Theodore and Becky arrived at the fork. Their ride to school together in the morning and the one back in the afternoon was really the only time during Theodore's school day when he was not threatened by the possibility of what might happen. The fifteen minutes either way with Becky was all that inspired the boy to tolerate the rest. And always, the iron bridge and Martha there to meet him was in the back of his mind. "Get through the day," he often told himself. "Just get through the day."

Mrs. Dirkmeyer had already begun checking papers when Theodore approached her desk and placed his on top of the few that had been turned in. The old teacher smiled up at the boy. "I'll get to yours next, Theodore," she said.

Theodore saw the red x's she was marking on the paper in front of her. He saw the name at the top of the page as he turned to go back to his desk. It was Bently Card's test paper, and from the looks of the marks Mrs. Dirkmeyer was decorating it with, Theodore could not imagine the boy coming through with a very good grade.

The teacher frowned as she wrote something at the bottom of Bently's test paper and laid it face down on the corner of her desk.

Theodore knew the one she picked up next was his. So did Becky, who was finishing up her exam two rows over and parallel to Theodore. She smiled and gave him a thumbs-up. A minute later, she rose and took her paper to the teacher's desk. A smile creased her lips as she watched the teacher mark Theodore's paper with an A+. Becky laid hers in the rack as the teacher joined her hands and spoke to the class.

"Well, I've just marked the first perfect paper of the day." She looked out over the class and then at Theodore. "There have been some good papers turned in, and so far, Theodore has scored the highest with a thoroughly perfect exam."

Some of the students who had finished their papers turned in their seats to look at the red-faced boy.

Theodore wanted to sink into his seat as he was

singled out. He immediately caught the scowl on Bently Card's face and two other boys who were his constant pals, Jerry Rust and Blue Daniels.

Theodore could not believe the teacher had done such a thing. Did she not understand that the special attention would work badly against him after class? Did she not understand how this bullying thing worked? Now he was marked. A marked boy who stood out like the dark mole on Mrs. Dirkmeyer's upper lip. This was serious. The last day of school, a perfect paper for him, and a barely passing grade for Bently. That was too much hot pepper in one bowl of soup, and the burn was going to come on quick.

Bently held up a folded piece of paper with his middle finger extended for Theodore's eyes only. He cut a glance at Jerry and Blue and raised his upper lip as if something stunk in the classroom. Then he turned around and slouched in his desk, his head back with his eyes closed. His body language said it all. Trouble was coming to Theodore Clatterbuck, and it would not be long in its arrival.

The end of science class was the end of the school day, and as the students filed out the door, Mrs. Dirkmeyer again congratulated Theodore and Becky, who had matched his score. "Great work, Theodore, Becky." She came close and put her arms around the two. "Have a great summer. I know I'll be hearing only good reports about you both next school year."

Bently was in earshot of the teacher's remarks. The anger in him caused his heart to pound with vengeance. The teacher's praise for Mayor Bloom's daughter, who would not give Bently the time of day was irritating to the ill-natured boy. But the resentment he felt for Theodore, the quirky son of a "shiftless farmhand," according to his father, was fueled further by the girl's interest and friendship with the boy. He hated them both. And more today than usual. Neither Jerry nor Blue was surprised when Bently collared them in the hallway.

"We're getting a ride out to Iron Bridge Road with Benny Jeter right now." Benny was Bently's older cousin who often drove the boys to and from school. "Just wait 'til he gets to that bridge." Bently sneered as he pushed the boys out the double doors and onto the sidewalk.

Becky saw the boys looking at her and Theodore as she stepped up onto the school bus, but thought no more about them. Theodore followed the girl onto the bus. He was surprised he had gotten that far without trouble. The bus door was pulled shut as Benny Jeter's souped-up Ford truck sped out of the school parking lot, throwing gravel as it fishtailed onto the highway. Fifteen minutes later, Becky and Theodore stepped off the school bus at the fork. There was not a cloud in the sky as they walked along.

"We nailed that science exam, didn't we?" Becky lifted her hands up, reaching for the sky. She felt light and free. "We've got the summer ahead of us, Theo. What adventures are you going to take me on?" The girl grabbed at a butterfly as it fluttered in front of her.

"Well," Theodore began with a look over his shoulder at the fork. "I thought we'd build us a raft and float to the old mill a mile or so downriver."

"Oh, I'd like that!" Becky brought her hands up to her chin and walked backwards just ahead of the boy. "We'll be river pirates and dress like Johnny Depp, or that old guy with the Rolling Stones."

Theodore laughed. "Yeah, or maybe not."

A car turned onto the bridge road from the fork. Theodore seemed nervous. He was relieved when he recognized the driver as Mrs. Horton. The woman waved as she passed the boy and girl.

"I wish we could sneak off to that treehouse we built summer before last." Becky's tone was serious. "But my mom says we can't do that anymore, now that I am a young lady, so to speak." She raised her eyebrow as she waited for the boy to respond.

"Yeah, well, I guess your mom's probably right, what with you being a 'young lady.' He scratched quotation marks in the air with his fingers to emphasize the description, "and me being a poor farm boy who mysteriously turns into a sex-crazed monster overnight."

Becky stopped and touched Theodore on the shoulder. "Don't think that way, Theo. She doesn't see you that way at all." The girl seemed sincere.

"Oh?" Theodore looked at Becky and then past her down the road where Martha would be waiting. "She doesn't, does she?"

Becky held back her answer for a moment, then confided, "Well, it's not the poor farm boy that bothers her," she said while smiling coyly. "It's the sex-crazed monster that really seems to cause her concern." The girl laughed out loud.

Theodore shook his head, smiling. "I know that

you're playing with me, Becky. But I do want you to know something." The boy had become serious.

Becky sensed the moment. She stepped close to Theodore and looked into his blue eyes. "What do you want me to know, Theo?" she asked softly.

Theodore had never known a girl like Becky Bloom. He figured that God did not make many like her. He looked at her standing there so close to him; he could smell the shampoo she had washed her hair with that morning. Her eyes were as dark as Martha's coat, and her pouting lips could widen into a fetching smile. For a moment, he wanted to kiss her. But he was not sure how to do it. In the moments their eyes filled with one another, the world seemed surreal to Theodore, like he was drifting between two dimensions. A free soul in one, and a captive in the other.

Finally, his words came slowly. "I want you to know that I like you more than I can tell you right now. And that I will always be good to you." The boy swallowed and continued, "I don't know why you like me, Becky, but I'm blessed for it. I am."

There was a tremble on the girl's lips as she responded. "You're blessed?" her voice emotional. "You listen to me, Theodore Clatterbuck. You are the best friend that I have ever had in my life. You get me like no one else. And one day..." She nodded her head and smiled through tearful eyes, "you just wait." She stood on her tiptoes and leaned into the boy. The gentle kiss she laid upon his lips was as sweet as honeysuckle and as sincere as an angel's promise.

The man Theodore would someday become fluttered in his heart like ripples on a still pool. And the bud of womanhood that urged the kiss from Becky settled in her eyes where Theodore found his reflection. Their little moment, so great in meaning, left them in a silence they could part with.

Theodore watched the girl safely down her driveway before he turned and headed toward the iron bridge and Martha. His worries had left him for now.

"I AIN'T SURE THIS IS A GOOD IDEA, Bently," Blue Daniels said as he tied a cord to the ring on Martha's collar and secured it to an iron bridge rail halfway across the one-lane bridge. He finished and attempted to pat the dog on the head. A low growl emitted from deep in Martha's throat and warned him away.

The Lab's good nature had permitted the boy to coax her to him from the other end of the bridge. But once in his hold and the cord tethered to her collar, she sensed a danger in him. Martha stood with the hair raised on her back and watched the boy's retreat. She threw a loud deep bark at him and growled again as he joined Bently Card and Jerry Rust at the end of the iron bridge.

"Don't worry about the dog," Bently snarled back. "It's out of the way now, and if a truck comes around the bend in the road up there fast enough, it might just end up as buzzard food."

Benny Jeter propped his head against the back-rest of the truck seat and took a long drag from his cigarette. He turned his head to the side and exhaled past the open window. He smirked and spat on the brown-stained gravel that was the surface of the old side road that he had backed his truck onto. Fifteen yards from the main road he could see what the boys were doing. He took another drag from his smoke and flipped it out the window. He stepped out of the truck and crushed the cigarette into the soft, dried earth with the heel of his shoe. Then he walked to the front of the truck and leaned back against the hood. "Is that nerd really worth the trouble, Bently?" he called looking at his wristwatch. "Come on, let's get out of here." He glanced around into the thick woods that lined the banks of the river. The afternoon sun drew long shadows through the hanging grapevines that clung to high limbs in the trees. The gurgle of the river flowing past rocks and log jams irritated the teenager. He would much prefer the loud rage of his truck engine and the searing blaze of dueling guitars in music that passed for country and pushed the ca-pacity of the speakers mounted in four places in his truck cab. "I ain't waitin' on you all afternoon," he threatened. "You best give this up and..."

"Quiet!" Bently waved off his cousin. "He's comin'." The boy looked at Jerry and Blue. "Get under the bridge," he commanded, "and have that rope ready when I call on ya."

The boys quickly disappeared and waited beside the stone and concrete abutment within earshot of Bently.

"Now, you stay quiet, Benny, and stay out of this. It's got nothin' to do with you." Bently's words were directed at his older cousin, but his eyes were trained up the road, where he saw Theodore appear around the bend.

Benny shook his head and walked back around to his truck door, where he leaned inside the window and grabbed his pack of cigarettes. "Don't get smart with me, you little snot. Without me, you got no way outta here after your little dance with Clatterbuck."

Bently Card ignored his cousin's reprimand. He was beyond a warning. He was past any advice that would have turned him away from his sick intention. All that was important to him now was to belittle, hurt, and shame the boy. The hatred that blazed through him singed the curtains of reason. The fact that the boy had never done anything to deserve Bently's wrath was lost in the abyss of darkness that terrorized the heart and soul of the son of a drunkard. Theodore Clatterbuck was Bently's muse. A diversion from the pits of his own sad and tragic life. Clatterbuck, a boy who came from nowhere. Poor and sickly. Odd and awkward in his movements. A joke on the playground. And yet, he possessed something that Bently had never known and could not yet even understand. For wisdom dwells in places beyond anger and self-loathing, and Bently Card had a long way to go on his course in life. Had he only realized that his anger, his blank and mindless fury with life, was a drawn veil to what he desired most. Acceptance. Then his young life would have not been such a tragic ordeal. For once a man recognizes the elements that color the worst in him, he is left with only one true recourse. And that is to color his life with the best of what he can find within himself.

Bently Card was not a man, and the time for wisdom was ahead for him. Sadly, he was caught in the present which set the stage for something he would forever regret.

Theodore heard Martha barking and stepped up his pace. He saw the boy standing at the entrance to the iron bridge and looking past him, he saw Martha. "What are you doing, Bently?" Theodore was almost out of breath as he posed his question. "Why have you tied my dog up to the bridge?" He started by the boy. "A car or truck could come around the bend in the road and…"

Bently stepped forward and pushed Theodore back with one hand. "Not so fast, Clatterbuck." He sneered.

Theodore smelled cigarette smoke and saw Benny Jeter watching from the side door of his truck, backed into the shade on the side road. Immediately he wondered where Jerry and Blue were. It was not Bently's nature to act alone.

Martha barked angrily and pulled at the rope that tethered her to the bridge.

Bently looked behind him at the struggling dog. "Aw, it's all worried about you. What's that like to have somebody, even a dog, to worry about you, huh?" Bently pushed Theodore, knocking a textbook from his hand.

"Better pick that up, Clatterbuck," he teased as he walked around the boy. "Don't want that nice science book to get dirty. It might hurt Miss Dungmeyer's feelings, and you don't want to do that now, do you?" He kicked the book as Theodore reached down to pick it up. "Oops," he laughed. "Tore a page. Better pick it up."

Theodore could feel his heart pounding in his chest. "Why are you doing this, Bently?" he asked, looking the boy in the eyes. "What have I done to you?"

Bently kicked the book again, harder this time. "You can't do nothin' to me, Clatterbuck." He raised his eyebrows as if he had an idea. "That is," he put up one finger, "except for the fact that you just irk the hell out of me." He shoved Theodore again, knocking the other books from the boy's hand. "I mean, you are just a poor, ragged little nothin' that shows up to school everyday, takin' up space and drawin' attention to yourself with good grades and a kind heart." Bently touched his chest mockingly. He looked at Theodore with disgust from head to toe. "Look at you, Clatterbuck. Nothin' fits you. Your sleeves are too short, and your britches are too high," he laughed. "What a pathetic nerd." He turned to the barking dog. "Shut up!" he shouted.

Martha pulled hard at the rope.

Theodore tried to move past Bently, but the boy reached out and tripped him. Theodore went down hard, his left cheek glancing on the gritty pavement of the road. Sand and grit crusted the blood that formed quickly on the wound as the boy struggled to rise.

"I don't think so," Bently said as he placed a foot in the center of Theodore's back and applied his weight.

The pressure to his back was too much for Theodore, and he went down. Agonized fear raced through him as he struggled at the feet of his persecutor.

"Come on up, boys!" Bently called. "Let's do this!"

On his command, Jerry and Blue came up from under the bridge.

Theodore saw Jerry holding a coil of rope in his hand. He raised his head and attempted to push himself up, but Bently's hold on him was too much.

Bently reached down and smacked him hard on the side of his face with an open hand. "Be still, Clatterbuck," he said as if possessed by the devil. "Slip the rope through his belt back here, Blue," Bently instructed. "Here, Jerry, throw this end up over that beam up there."

Jerry did as he was told, not daring to oppose his leader.

Quickly Bently tied a hard knot and suddenly stood up. "Come on!" he yelled to the two boys. "Pull!"

The three boys grabbed the rope and started for the end of the bridge. In seconds, Theodore was ten feet in the air, dangling from the back of his belt. The pain was so severe, he could not call out. Breathing was difficult. The rope lowered a bit as the boys held the tension and came back to the bridge where they quickly tied it off.

Bently Card laughed aloud as he watched the helpless boy swing back and forth above the bridge entrance. He wiped his hands on his jeans. "There now, Clatterbuck," he taunted, "you just hang around for a while." He motioned for Benny to bring the truck.

"We're not gonna leave him up there, are we, Bently?" Blue's tone was serious. He looked over at Jerry, who would not meet his eyes. Blue continued over the roar of Benny's truck engine. "We can't leave him up there, guys," he pleaded. "I heard he's got a heart condition, or somethin'."

"Shut up, Blue." Bently was irritated. He opened the truck door and waited. "Are you comin' or not?" he asked.

Jerry jumped into the cab and scooted over next to Benny, who seemed anxious to leave.

"Come on, you snits," Benny blurted out. "You're lucky nobody uses this road much. Let's get outta here."

"But...," Blue started. He looked up at Theodore and saw the strain in the boy's face, his bulging eyes.

"Okay, Blue." Bently stepped up into the truck and closed the door. "You stay here and take the heat. We're outta here."

Benny revved the engine and thrust the gearstick into first.

"You tell anybody who put you up there, Clatterbuck, and I swear I'll finish you," Bently hollered out the threat.

"What about the dog?" Jerry asked.

Bently laughed. "Hey, maybe it'll chew through the rope and then save its master."

Blue looked up at Theodore again.

"Get in the truck, Blue!" demanded Bently.

"I'm sorry, Theodore." Blue's apology could hardly be heard over the truck's engine, and the boy barely grabbed the tailgate as Benny accelerated.

Theodore listened as the truck sped away. And then, for minutes after that, he swung back and forth, helpless and in pain.

Martha barked without end while pulling at the rope that held her, until finally, the ring on her collar gave way, and she was freed. Immediately, she ran to Theodore and began jumping and pacing beneath him. Her desperate barks were intermingled with helpless whines.

Theodore could hardly breathe and began to drift in and out of consciousness. "Becky," he said aloud. "Get Becky!" he cried. "Go, Martha," he finally commanded as loud as he could. "Go get Becky!"

Martha looked up the road and back at Theodore.

"Get Becky." Theodore's last command was only a strained whisper. But it was enough. The dog obeyed.

Theodore could hear the pads of her paws against the gritty pavement as she left him. For another minute, the boy hung there, suspended in misery, until the pain at his hips turned to numbness. His breaths were short and raspy. And his heart pounded into his throat. The vessels in his neck and at his temple bulged from the pressure and strain on his body. He could hear the wind in the trees along the river and the slurping of the water around rocks and falls as he felt himself drifting away into a place of light and open space. The echo of Martha's bark beckoned him past the realm of his consciousness. He could feel the bonds of his limitations lifting as he stepped into a field of golden flowers. Familiar voices rode on the warm, gentle breeze that pushed the flowers as if they were sparkling swells on an ocean. He walked in this waist-high beauty for a long time, guided only by the distant barking of Martha, until finally he tired, lay down, closed his eyes, and slept.

BECKY BLOOM WAS UNEASY as she rode her bike down the driveway to the main road. Thirty minutes ago she had left Theodore standing at the entrance as she walked home. Those last moments there with him had been so special to her, and she had walked home as if on a cloud. Her fondness for the boy and a shared discovery of their young hearts had endeared him to the girl, even more than she could understand at her age. No matter what might happen in their futures, Theodore would always hold a place in her heart. *He could be the one,* she thought. But even if he was not, he would remain a part of her.

Becky had heard Martha's bark as soon as she opened her bedroom window. That was unusual. The dog was typically quiet. The only time she would bark was if something was out of the norm to her.

Becky had quickly changed her clothes and was now peddling her bike as fast as she could. She stopped at the road and waited for a truck that was coming down the hill from the fork. She recognized the driver at once. It was David Horton. He stopped his truck at the Bloom driveway.

"Howdy, Becky." The old man was always in a good mood and was not stingy with a smile.

"Hi, Mr. Horton." Becky seemed anxious. David Horton perceived her mood. He had known the girl all her life, and it was a usual thing for her to take the time to chat with him.

"You're in a mighty big hurry comin' down that driveway this afternoon. It's a good thing you didn't get out on the road sooner."

"Oh? Why is that?" the girl was puzzled.

The man pushed back his straw hat and scratched his head before he answered. "Well, I just passed Benny

Jeter and a truckload of boys speeding up past the fork. I figured they came from down here. You see 'em?"

"Oh, no!" Becky's voice was frantic. She threw her bike down and ran around to the passenger side of the old farmer's truck. She opened the door and climbed in. "We've got to get down to the bridge fast, Mr. Horton." She slammed the door as she scooted up on the seat. "They've done something to Theo. I know they have."

David Horton did not need convincing. He knew of the trouble the boy had at school with Bently Card. And he knew that Benny Jeter was Card's cousin. He was almost sure he had seen Bently in the white Ford truck as it sped by him minutes ago. "Hold on, Becky," he advised as he was about to press down on the accelerator. "Ain't that Martha coming up the road?"

The girl jumped out of the truck and met the Lab, but as she tried to calm her, Martha turned and headed back down the road. "Martha!" the girl called.

The Lab turned around, but only for a second before barking and running back down the road toward the bridge.

"Come on and get in the truck, Becky," David Horton called out the window. "She wants us to follow her."

Martha was disappearing around the bend in the road as the farmer gave his truck the gas. Seconds later, they rounded the bend in the road and were able to see down to the bridge. The truck was gaining on Martha when Becky looked past her and recognized, to her horror, what the Lab was trying to relate.

"Oh, no!" she screamed. "Oh, my God! No, no, no," she cried, a hand to her mouth. "Look what they have done to him," she sobbed.

David Horton did not try to calm the girl. There was no time for it. Instead, he sped to the bridge and slammed on the brakes. His quick eyes sized up the situation as he got out of the truck and approached Theodore. Immediately the old man went to the bridge rail and untied the rope. He wrapped it around his back as he braced himself. "Hold him as I let him down, Becky." He fought back the lump in his throat as he instructed the girl. "Take him gently, now. We don't want him to be hurt anymore than he is." The man began lowering the boy slowly and carefully.

"I got you, Theo," Becky cried as she reached up and touched the boy's limp hands, pulling him into her arms.

Seconds later, a tear creased David Horton's cheek as he heard the girl plead to God to let him live.

A ROLL OF THUNDER IN THE DISTANCE awoke the boy. A lick on his cheek from Martha brought a smile to his lips. Theodore sat up. "Martha," he said quietly.

The excited Lab could not love him enough. Theodore laughed and fell over on her, his face buried in her shiny coat. They tumbled and played in the shadows of the golden flowers until thunder rolled again in the far distance.

Theodore stood up. "Where are we, girl?" he asked, expecting no answer. "I've never been here before that I can remember." He looked down at the Lab and then behind them. There were golden flowers as far as he could see. Puzzled, the boy began to walk in the direction of the storm. "We've got to get home, girl."

Martha walked beside and sometimes just ahead of her human, but never did she stray, for the field of flowers was also a mystery to her.

"Mama will be wondering where we are, girl. She'll want to hear about my science test today. And dad, he'll be finishing up that lower field and needs me to help him drop some seed." The boy stood and looked around him. "I don't see anything but flowers, Martha." He walked on. "I know we've never been here before, and I'm not sure which direction to go."

Suddenly Theodore caught a whiff of rain on the breeze that came out of the eastern sky. He could see the shower coming in the distance like a misty veil. "We're about to get wet, Martha." He sat down on a flat rock and pulled the Lab close to him. "Dad will be happy with this."

The shower did not last long and soon disappeared altogether, leaving behind a cleanness in the air. The golden flowers seemed even more fragrant now to Theodore. The honeybees he just began to notice buzzed about the flower tops. They tilted the golden flowers with their weight. The boy arose and studied the eastern sky. Martha wandered out from him a short distance, sniffing the air and ground. She stopped often to look back at Theodore, anticipating his call.

The sun was behind the boy as he watched colors forming in the sky to the east. "A rainbow," he whispered to himself. "Look, Martha!" he called out. "Look at how close that rainbow is to us."

By now, the colors were forming into a vivid spectacle unlike anything Theodore had ever seen. Even the Lab seemed to notice the gigantic arch in the sky.

"If I could only touch it," Theodore spoke aloud to himself. "If I could, then I know something miraculous would happen." He began walking toward the beautiful arch in the sky. "Come on, girl!" he called to Martha.

The Lab reined in close and paced herself just ahead of the boy.

At first Theodore walked slowly, but as the colors of the rainbow intensified, his pace quickened until he was in an all-out run. He never felt better or more alive in his life. It was as if the beauty of the flowers and the colored sky had given him energy he had never known. Martha powered through the sea of flowers, her satiny ears flopping like bird wings.

Boy and dog ran together for what seemed the longest time until finally Theodore slowed to catch his breath. A small tree, a white-petaled dogwood, appeared on the rise, and the boy moved toward it. His heart was now beating at an accelerated rate, and he gasped for air as he reached the tree and leaned against the cool bark of its trunk. Filtered sunlight dappled the boy's blonde hair. Theodore's side ached as he slumped to his knees. Martha came to his side and nudged him into a sitting position, his back against the tree trunk, and his legs out straight. When the boy had found comfort, the Lab lay down beside him, her head resting on his lap. Minutes passed before Theodore could speak.

"Well, we chased it, didn't we, girl?" he finally asked. "And look." He raised his hand and pointed. "It doesn't look any closer than before. Isn't that funny?" Theodore felt exhausted. The burst of energy he had felt before was spent. His heart was pounding in his chest. "Calm down," he told it in a whisper.

Martha licked the boy's hand. She could hear his heart beating. She sensed his nature.

Theodore looked at the beautiful rainbow again before his sight dimmed, and he closed his eyes. He patted Martha's head. "If we could have caught it, girl," he forced his eyelids open for one last look at the rainbow, "we could have explored its mystery. I could tell Dad something that maybe he's forgotten. Who really knows what's in a rainbow, anyway?" He closed his eyes and minutes passed on the warm breeze that carried the boy's whispers beyond the rainbow to a faraway place, where they filled the sails of a waiting ship and the ears and heart of an ancient wind sailor.

AT FIRST MARTHA'S BARKING seemed distant to Theodore, almost as if she were in a cave. They echoed in his mind, and for a moment, while he drifted in between the dream state and consciousness, he resisted an inclination to open his eyes and call out. But suddenly the echoing subsided, and the deep-throated barks of the Lab jolted the boy's eyes open.

"Martha!" he called out instantly.

Immediately, the dog barked from behind him. Theodore leaned to the side and looked. His eyes widened as he quickly stood up and walked out from under the dogwood tree. Martha stood her ground a dozen feet away, the hair bristled across her shoulders, her eyes trained on the sight her human only now discovered.

"A ship?" Theodore questioned.

"Ah. The *Wind Sailor* ain't just a ship, lad," a voice came from behind him.

Theodore turned around and was stunned at the sight of the man who answered him. He tried, but could not speak. Even Martha ceased her barking at the sound of the man's voice.

"She's a schooner, fast and agile in the wind, she is."

Theodore tried to form the word "who" but was only successful in puckering his lips. His voice just could not follow the breath that began the question he struggled to ask.

The man perceived the boy's predicament and stepped forward. "The name is Roy G. Biv, lad. And I'm the captain of this fine vessel that awaits yer boarding."

"But, but...," Theodore managed the word twice as

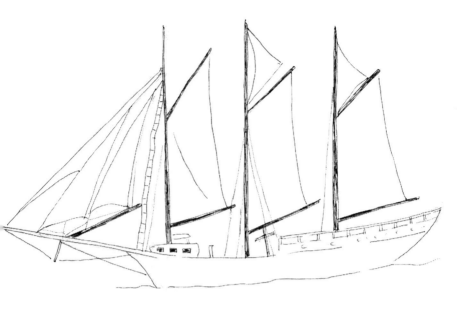

the man walked closer to him and extended his hand. Hesitantly, he reached out and felt the warm and firm grip of the captain's hand. The boy's mouth was open as his eyes swept over the man.

Old, but not ancient, the man who called himself a captain was a pinch shorter than Theodore, which brought him a good two inches below six feet in height. He was thin of body, yet well-proportioned, with broad shoulders and good posture. His face was handsome in a rugged way. It seemed chiseled and wind burned. There were some creases above his brow and around his mouth and at the corners of his deep set eyes, which seemed to change from sky blue to indigo in a blink. Silver hair with bluish streaks fell onto the collar of his ragged blue waistcoat and swept back over his ears like ruffs of feathers. Milky pearls and colored beads adorned the braids of hair that started behind

his ears and clung to his lapels. Shell necklaces matted
his chest and spilled from his half-buttoned linen shirt,
which was also ragged and open at the wrists. High-
waist canvas britches fit to a tee, flared at the thighs and
then gathered below his knees, where
each leg was tucked into high
boots that were black and
scuffed. A pearl-handled
Bowie knife, unsheathed,
was tucked firmly under
a thick, dark belt with an
oversize gold buckle.

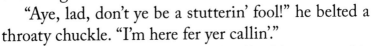

"Aye, lad, don't ye be a stutterin' fool!" he belted a
throaty chuckle. "I'm here fer yer callin'."

"My calling?" Theodore was finally able to voice his
disbelief.

"Aye," the captain responded. "'Tis what I do.
Answer the call from them like ye, who fer wish or
dream, desire the truth o' the rainbow."

"But I...," Theodore started.

The man waved his hand and stepped past the boy
toward the vessel that seemed to be floating just above
the golden flowers.

Theodore touched the crown of Martha's head.
The dog now stood close beside him and watched the
man walk past. "I thought a schooner was smaller
than that, with fewer sails." The boy was awed by the
ship.

Suddenly a thick rope ladder was flung over the
portside of the vessel, and Theodore saw the head and
shoulders of a small man. "Who's that?" he asked.

The little man secured the ladder, then stood on a stool so that he was visible from his waist up.

"The name's Birdie Wiggins, lad." He tipped his head. "First mate and cook of this here vessel." He shook his head and winked at the captain, who had started up the ladder.

From where Theodore stood, Birdie was an odd looking individual. The boy noticed the scarf around his head that fluttered in the breeze and his collarless river shirt, frazzled at the wrists. He wore a dark vest over the shirt and a thick, black belt with an oversize brass buckle. His baggy linen britches were bunched at the waist. Theodore could not see the man below his knees.

Captain Biv threw a leg over the gunnel and slipped onto the deck of the vessel. He slapped Birdie on the shoulder proudly. "Thar's never been a finer first mate or ship's cook than Birdie, here."

Birdie smiled and pulled a short-stem pipe from his vest pocket. He clenched it between his stained teeth and shook the ladder with his hands. "Come aboard now, lad, and bring yer furry friend. Thar's no time to tarry."

Theodore looked around him and then down at Martha. He looked back up at the captain and Birdie. "Where are we?" he asked.

The captain laughed. "Why, yer in a field of flowers what's as vast as an ocean. 'Tis a perty place, fer sure, but after a while, ye'll be walkin' in circles."

"You mean, there's nothing else here but flowers and bees and that tree?"

The captain glanced at his first mate, then urged the little man over the gunnel and down the rope ladder.

"Let Birdie thar help y'ens on deck, lad, and then I'll tell ye some tales as we chase yer rainbow."

Theodore knelt down and patted Martha's chest. "We got nowhere else to go, girl."

Martha looked up at the schooner and whined a little.

"And besides," the boy continued, "this is too good to pass up." Theodore was surprised when Birdie gently gathered Martha into his short, strong arms.

"Climb on up the ladder, lad, and ye and the cap'n can hoist this lady on deck."

Theodore climbed up the rope with little trouble and was helped over the gunnel by Captain Biv. In the time it took for him to turn around and look down, Birdie had wrapped the Lab securely into the rope ladder, tied it, and given the signal for the captain and Theodore to bring her up. The little man waited patiently while the dog was attended to. Once Martha was set free on deck, she shook her head, flopping her ears and then began sniffing around.

The captain tossed the ladder back over the portside and called, "Come on up, Birdie."

When the first mate climbed over the gunnel, he brought up the ladder and hoisted the anchor from the flowers. Immediately the schooner began to drift along above the flower heads.

When the captain was satisfied, he walked to the helm of the schooner. "Good then, Birdie," he called.

"Tighten the jib sail, and me and our new shipmate will tack her and be off with the wind."

Theodore followed the captain, careful of his footing, as the ship seemed to be moving beneath his footsteps.

"Aye," called Birdie as he tightened the sail and tied it off. "'Tis done, Cap'n."

"You are going to tack her?" Theodore asked as he took his place beside Captain Biv at the big steering wheel.

"*That's what he said*," a young lady's voice answered the boy.

Startled, Theodore looked around. "There was no one else near him.

"*I'm down here*," the voice came again.

Theodore looked down and saw only Martha beside him. "Martha?" he questioned.

"*Yes.*" The Lab could speak without even moving her mouth.

Flabbergasted, Theodore looked over at Captain Biv. "Am I...? Can she...?" He shook his head and waited.

The captain smiled. "No, yer not losin' yer marbles, lad. Yer just hearin' the thoughts of yer pet. 'Tis a normal thing aboard the *Wind Sailor.*"

Theodore looked down at Martha. "Really? But, but...," he started.

"Well, let's just say thar's some wonders aboard this ship," the captain spoke as he turned the steering wheel hard, bringing the bow of the schooner to face the wind. Immediately the sails filled, and the booms creaked and shifted. "Remember that as ye sail with us, lad, or ye might get a boom on yer head." The captain smiled and called out to his first mate. "Let's start the chase fer the lad, Birdie. That rainbow he's wantin' is a beauty if I ever saw one."

The little man waved back at the captain and walked to the bow of the vessel, where he stood next to the foremast, his ruddy face to the wind.

Theodore cautiously walked over to portside and looked down. The golden fields were far beneath them now, as the vessel rose into the sky, past wings of shallow clouds. "Look, Martha!" he called out, "we're flying!"

"Sailin', lad," corrected Captain Biv. "Yer wind sailin'."

Martha jumped up, her paws over the gunnels and ears flapping in the wind. *"You think they have a parachute handy in case of a spill?"* she asked.

Theodore laughed. "I don't know, Martha." He faced the wind and lifted his arms out like wings. "All I know is we're on a ship called the *Wind Sailor*, with Captain Roy G. Biv and his first mate. We're flying in the sky and chasing that rainbow over there." He pointed. Then he bent down and hugged the Lab. "And I can hear you, Martha. I can hear anything you want to say."

Martha licked the boy's cheek, then broke away from his embrace and moved toward the bow of the ship and the little man standing there.

Birdie was pleased that the dog came and sat down beside him. "Ah, yer a good friend to the lad, Martha," he spoke as he tickled the nape of her neck.

Martha did not mind. But she was concerned for her human. *"He's all I've got, Birdie,"* the Lab opened her thoughts to the little man. *"But I'm not all he has. His mother and father would never be the same without him. And Becky..."* Martha looked away and then back at Birdie. *"Well, he has a place in her heart that is bigger than she can even realize right now. His life has not been easy, but there are a lot of people who like and respect him, although he doesn't believe it. I'm not sure what he hopes to find in that rainbow he's been chasing all his life, but I'm here to see it with him. And he will remember that if he comes back, won't he?"* Hope colored the words of Martha's thoughts.

Birdie knew this. "When they come to us, them who's dreamin' or wishin' on a rainbow, we take 'em to the colors. They're like seas in the air that come and go. The different colors speak to 'em when we sail on 'em and teaches 'em to know better the things that confuse 'em. With each one, it's different, but worth the voyage." Birdie looked up at the full sails of the schooner, then back into Martha's eyes. "Don't ye fret none 'bout yer human, Martha," he answered her. "Just enjoy the journey we're startin'."

The Lab got up and walked back to the helm where Theodore was standing beside the captain.

"The sails have turned blue, like the sky, Captain Biv. They were gold when I first saw them in the flower field."

The captain smiled as he leaned back in his tall chair. "Ye have a good eye 'bout ye, lad. By now yer prob'ly figurin' the old *Wind Sailor* kin change her

55

color to match her surroundin's. And yer right 'bout that. 'Tis a peculiar thing, fer sure, but necessary. Fer if it weren't possible, then thar'd be lots o' folks askin' questions 'bout her voyages."

"Oh?" Theodore was intrigued. "So, she's invisible? Are we invisible, also?"

"Well now," the captain chuckled. "Be sure that the *Wind Sailor* exists, lad. Fer yer here, ain't ye?" He looked seriously at the boy and raised his bushy brow. "One might see us from below as a discoloration in the sky, or as a swift-moving cloud. Ye might even see it as a figment of yer imagination. But then thar is them who believe it, so that when they're asked aboard, they come."

"Like me," Theodore said proudly. "Me and Martha."

"Aye, lad. Like ye and yer pet." Captain Biv looked down at the Lab as she took her place next to her human. He dug in his jacket pocket for a pipe, and when he found it, he brought it out and placed it in the corner of his mouth. A few puffs and tobacco smoke drifted past his ears.

Theodore was amazed the man could pull a lighted pipe out of his pocket. "How did you do that?" he asked, very amused.

The captain smiled, showing his perfectly white teeth. "As I told ye before, lad, thar's wonders to be seen when yer aboard the *Wind Sailor* with Captain Roy G. Biv and his first mate, Birdie Wiggins. Thar's wonders, fer sure!"

Theodore smiled and looked down at Martha. The captain was right.

IN THE REALM OF THE RAINBOW there are wonders that stretch the imagination from one possibility to the next. Fact or fiction have no place here, for the realm itself borders a place in the mind where things are perceived that we could never accept within the bland reality in which we must live our lives. Therefore, when one takes exit from the world for periods of time, misunderstood by most and for reasons that vary, it is often a holiday for that individual and a stressful period for those awaiting their return. Theodore Clatterbuck was unaware of the concern that surrounded his journey. For to realize it would have snapped him back far too soon.

The Red Sea

"THAR 'TIS, LAD!" Captain Biv walked to the beam of the schooner and turned starboard. "Watch how the colors play upon the sails of the *Wind Sailor*. Seas in the sky, drawin' at us, hopin' to be sailed, yearnin' fer an adventure and maybe, a sharin' of what it holds." The captain put his hand on Theodore's shoulder. "That's yer rainbow, lad. Now, are ye willin' to sail its colors?"

Theodore looked over at Birdie Wiggins, who stood at the gunnel, stone-faced and waiting.

Martha stood close to her human and stared at the rainbow. She licked the moist air that sprayed out from its loose band of colors.

Theodore was amazed at the size of the arch. Its distant perfection had now become hazy and undefined. He could hardly believe the size of the color bands, or "seas," according to the captain.

The wind this close to the rainbow was such that Birdie lowered the sails to avoid the possibility of the *Wind Sailor* being pulled into the belching turbulence of the Red Sea.

The captain shouted over the howl of the wind. "Are ye willin', lad, or do we turn back? Say it, and I'll give the order!"

Theodore leaned into the gusts and walked to the

starboard and placed his hands firmly on the gunnel, bracing himself against the wind. For a moment he stood there, until finally, the fear that had taken his voice gave way to the challenge of his true spirit, and he turned and shouted his desire. "Go for it, Captain!" he called out. "Let's ride the seas in the sky and discover their treasures!"

Captain Biv grinned and shouted the command. "Raise the sails, Birdie. We're goin' in!"

"Come on, lad!" shouted the now smiling first mate. "I'll raise the mainsail, and ye tend to the jib. We'll meet at the beam and hoist the others. Watch them booms as we go, 'cause we're goin' to a treacherous place, fer sure!"

Red sails came up as the boy and Birdie worked, while the captain led Martha to the stern to take a place next to his chair.

Captain Biv used all his strength to steady the schooner until the fisher sail and the staysail were raised. He then leaned forward and steered hard into the arch of the rainbow, and the turbulence that bordered its colors.

A distant onlooker would have never noticed the schooner or its challenged effort to gain entry onto the red sky sea, but those on deck of the *Wind Sailor* held fast for their lives for the duration of the time it took to settle onto the long rolling swells that occasionally capped and slapped at the schooner's starboard.

The captain found the eye of the wind and pulled the bow of the vessel into it. "Watch the booms," he warned above the wind and swells.

Theodore ducked his head as he made his way to the bow of the ship.

"Look!" Birdie shouted from the beam of the schooner. Theodore looked in the direction the little man was pointing. There he saw the silhouette of an imposing vessel, its sails blowing in the wind. There was no doubt the ship, tall and fast, was gaining on them.

"What is it, Birdie?" Theodore shouted.

"It ain't a good thing, lad," Birdie answered. "That's

our old nemesis, Split Nose Mary, the meanest and ugliest pirate what ever wore a corset, and her crew of headless swordsmen, comin' in on us in a hurry, as to plunder and aggravate us."

"You mean this has happened before?" Theodore could not believe his luck. Pirates in a rainbow was the last thing he would have imagined finding in the Red Sea. But then, he had never really imagined the Red Sea of a rainbow.

Birdie made his way to the stern of the schooner, and Theodore followed. "Before and after," responded the first mate. "Mary's always trollin' these waters fer the challenge of a mean encounter. She's got a lot of feistiness in her, and she kin sail that galleon as well as any man." Birdie looked to the captain for his command. "Ye best hold onto somethin', lad, fer this is whar things gets tricky."

Theodore hugged the mainmast and called to Martha. The Lab quickly found her way to the boy and took her place close to his legs. Sea spray gathered in trickles on Theodore's face. He wiped his eyes and spotted the bulging sails of the galleon as it appeared behind a massive swell. Astonished at the sudden nearness of the dark ship, the boy winced and shouted at the captain. "She's almost on us, Captain Biv!"

With a hard turn of the wheel, the captain swung the schooner to starboard and avoided what would have certainly been a collision the smaller ship could not have withstood, for the bow of Split Nose Mary's galleon was a massive blade of timber more than capable of cutting the schooner in half.

Theodore sank to his knees in fear in the passing shadow of the ship. Martha lunged forward and barked savagely as a dark object flew close to her.

"Watch them swordsmen, lad," warned the captain. "They're apt to rip our sails and snatch a thing or two in passin'."

Above him Theodore saw the headless swordsmen. Three of them swung from the ends of ropes out from the galleon. They flew through the air like ragged vultures, caught in a downwind, sounding their bloodcurdling cries and lashing out with their swords.

Theodore tried to move, but fear held him to his knees. He watched helplessly as Birdie ran about trying his best to thwart the swordsmen with a hooked pole. Finally, the first mate let out a loud holler as he caught the rope swing of one of the swordsmen and gave it such a yank that the hapless creature was flung off the end of his rope and far out into the red swells. "Thar ye go, ye brainless mucker," he laughed. "Take ye a little swim back to yer mama!"

Two more swordsmen shrieked their terrifying cries as their flying bodies displaced the air close to the schooner's portside. The jib sail was slashed by one swordsman as the other one swung in low for a try at the mainsail. But as the ragged creature was about to expend his energy to no good, a strong arm reached upward and the broad blade of a Bowie knife flashed in the trickle of sunlight and severed the rope just above the bony fingers of the hideous creature. The headless swordsman fell hard onto the deck of the schooner, rolled and slammed into the gunnel, where he lay crippled like a ragged scarecrow. A portside tilt rolled him over the deck to the man who stopped him.

Captain Biv stuck his Bowie blade back into its place behind his belt and while still holding the steering wheel with his left hand, reached over and grabbed the headless creature by the strap of his sword sheath, and with a mighty effort, flung it hard against the galleon's side as it passed.

Split Nose Mary screamed her anger and shook her sword at the captain as she looked down from her place behind the ship's wheel and heard the thud against the hull of her ship. She was about to fling a curse when instead, a smile creased her thin, crusty lips. "Bring it aboard, Itchy," she laughed. "I'll have that one bringing me my slippers by mornin'."

Martha yelped in pain as the larger of the swordsmen, and the only one left to mayhem, reached down and grabbed the dog by the scruff of the neck then swung hard back toward the galleon.

"No!" Theodore screamed. In an instant the fear that had brought the boy to his knees left him. The moment he saw Martha hoisted into the air, he rose and ran as hard as he could.

"Grab her, lad!" shouted Birdie from where he stood at the bow of the schooner.

But Theodore did not hear the first mate, nor did he have the first concern for his own safety. All he had, both physically and mentally, was directed at saving Martha from the clutches of a foe he had little time to fear.

Captain Biv watched with wide-open eyes as the boy jumped upon the gunnel of the schooner and sprang out into the narrow corridor between the two passing vessels. The old sailor shouted his approval and amazement when with both hands, Theodore grasped the end of the rope he had just severed and swung hard up and over the side of the galleon.

"Take this, lad!" Captain Biv called out, and with a mighty throw of his hand, the Bowie knife sank deep into a beam in front of where Theodore landed on the ship's deck. The adrenaline flowing through the boy allowed easy removal of the wide blade and immediately he ran about severing ropes and slashing sails.

Split Nose Mary screamed, "Get him!" But the only ruffian left, Itchy, was in no hurry to take on the boy who charged about the ship, fearless and challenging. The cowering swordsman pushed the growling Martha toward Mary and ran to the ladder that led up to the ship's crow's nest. In the second it would have taken for him to blink an eye, had he had one to blink, he was sitting high above the ship's deck and away from Theodore's wrath.

"There now, creature," Mary's voice was like a witch's attempt at goodness. "Come to Mary," she coaxed.

Martha growled and backed away, and when she saw Theodore, she ran to him. She lapped at the boy's face as he knelt to greet her.

Mary stood watching among fallen sails and severed ropes. "My ship," she whined. "Look what you've done

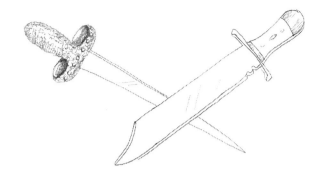

to my ship." Mary's long, unbridled hair blew around her face and mouth as she accused the boy.

Theodore stood up and walked over to her.

Mary pulled her sword and pointed it at him. "Who are you?" she demanded. "Who are you to come aboard my ship and tear it to pieces?"

Theodore knocked the sword aside with the thick blade of Captain Biv's Bowie knife. Unafraid, he stepped closer to the pirate witch. "My name is Theodore Clatterbuck," he replied without a blink of his eyes. "And don't you ever lay a hand on my dog again."

The pirate witch raised her ugly chin, stepped back and returned her sword to its scabbard. "I'll remember you, Theodore Clatter...Buck," she snarled.

"And I, you, Split Nose Mary. You and everyone like you." Theodore turned from the wretched woman and walked to the gunnel of the ship. He looked over and saw the *Wind Sailor* floating in the now calm Red Sea.

"Ere ye all right, lad?" called the captain from his place at the wheel.

Theodore waved down at him.

"Tie yer dog in a sling and lower her down. Birdie and I will fetch her in."

The boy cut the needed rope with the Bowie and complied. Minutes later, Martha was safely back aboard the *Wind Sailor*, and Theodore was about to step over the side and leave the galleon.

"Yer ship is small, boy," Mary spoke from her chair at the helm of the great galleon that lurked in the water next to the schooner.

Theodore sat on the gunnel of the big ship and looked down at the schooner, its captain and first mate. Then he turned back to the pirate witch and smiled. "Yes, but in a few minutes the wind will catch our sails and we'll be gone on our way, while you will be here, dead calm on the sea." With that the boy lowered himself over the side of the ship and soon stood again on the deck of the schooner.

When finally the *Wind Sailor* was far enough away from the galleon, Birdie and Theodore lifted the sails.

"Don't ye fret none, Mary," called Captain Biv turning to the Orange Sea and watching his sails fill. "Me and Birdie'll find ye on our way back and help ye with yer riggin's."

Split Nose Mary nodded her head slowly as she watched her old friend sail away. "Come on down, Itchy," she called up to the crow's nest. "Let's lower the life boat and find yer brothers. I'm sure they're bobbin' out there somewhere."

The ragged swordsman came down gingerly from his perch. "Kin I unbutton this now, Mary?" he asked as he approached the woman.

Mary nodded, and the little man poked his head up through the open neck hole of his shirt.

Itchy took a deep breath and blinked his eyes as if to bring them back into focus. He stood next to Mary at the ship's gunnel and watched the *Wind Sailor* ride the swells toward the Orange Sea. "I envy the lad's coming adventures, Mary," spoke the little man. "A safe journey to ye, Theodore Clatterbuck." Itchy's well-wishing was barely audible, although Mary perceived his sincerity. She smiled. "The risks of the journey are worth the lessons learned, Itchy." She patted the man on his shoulder.

Itchy grinned and nodded his head. He reached out and began lowering the lifeboat. There were familiar voices calling from the Red Sea. "We best find me brothers and haul 'em in, Mary."

The pirate chuckled. "Yes, they really went out of their way on this one."

The Orange Sea

MARTHA ENJOYED THE ATTENTION shown her by Theodore in the hours since her exciting rescue. As she was busy gnawing on a large ham bone that he gave her, courtesy of Birdie, she looked up at her human. *"Thank you for saving me, Theodore,"* her thought came to the boy in words audible only in his mind.

Theodore pulled the Lab close to him. "I couldn't lose you, Martha," he answered softly. "Not like that."

"You were brave, Theodore." Martha rested her jaw on Theodore's knee.

The boy smiled. "Yeah, I guess I was."

Birdie Wiggins could not help overhearing the conversation between the Lab and Theodore as he stood tying off the last stitch in the jib sail slit by one of the headless swordsmen. In the realm of the rainbow, animal thoughts are heard by all.

"Aye, Martha," the first mate agreed. "'Tis a dreadful thought of what might've become of ye, had the lad not acted." Birdie stood up and hoisted the jib. When he had finished and tied off the rope, he looked seriously at Theodore. "'Twas fer sure a brave thing ye did, lad." He waved at the boy. "And me and the Cap'n are thinkin' that it were jest 'bout the most excitin' rescue we ever saw."

Theodore looked intently at the first mate. "You

mean you and the captain have dealt with Split Nose Mary before?" He stood up as he posed his question.

Birdie looked back at the helm where Captain Biv sat. "Well, we've had a few run-ins with her in passin'," he laughed. "But never that close."

Suddenly, and in no effort to camouflage his dodging of the subject of Split Nose Mary, the first mate walked quickly toward the bow of the schooner. "Look thar!" he called, pointing his finger. "See whar the red waters merge with the yeller and forms the Orange Sea?"

Theodore and Martha followed the man as he spoke.

"Them waters is calmer than the Red Sea. 'Tis a cheerful sea, the Orange one. Not as deep as the Red, but challengin' in its own ways."

Theodore stood next to Birdie at the bow of the schooner. He could sense the calmness as the *Wind Sailor* passed through a sunlit mist and entered the Orange Sea. Immediately he felt different, more at ease. He smelled the air. It was sharp and fragrant, like citrus. His mouth watered with the thought of fruit.

"Look, Birdie." Theodore was amazed. "The sails have changed color from red to orange."

"Aye, lad," Birdie agreed. "'Tis the norm on the seas of the rainbow."

"What will we find here?" Theodore leaned against the gunnel and looked out over the rolling swells.

The voice that answered him was that of Captain Biv, who had left his place at the helm, trading places with his first mate. The captain patted Martha on her head and joined the boy at the bow of the ship. "Oh, ye never quite know what's in store fer ye in the Orange Sea, lad. Me and Birdie has passed o'er it fer ages, and thar's always somethin' new unfoldin'. Look thar ahead." The captain pointed a crooked finger.

Theodore searched through an orange mist and saw what looked like a small island with a shallow beachhead and a green interior. "An island?" he questioned, looking at Captain Biv. "Is that an island ahead of us?"

"Aye, lad," the captain answered. "'Tis the Island of the Rue."

"The Rue?"

"Aye," replied the captain, his face turned up toward the sun's haze. "Smell the air. 'Tis the green leaves of the woody plants bearin' fruit and medicines."

"You've been there before?" Theodore asked as the *Wind Sailor* approached the island.

Captain Biv nodded his head. "Aye, a time or two. Thar's a maiden thar, perty as the yeller flowers that adorn the trees. Her name is Aurum."

"A maiden?" Theodore could hardly believe that a woman would live on an island in the middle of a sea in a rainbow. But then, he thought to himself, *who would have imagined a pirate witch on the Red Sea?*

"Aurum." Theodore said the name.

Minutes later the boy helped Birdie lower the sails as the captain steered the schooner into a hidden cove.

Birdie dropped the anchor, then the captain called the order. The misty breeze brought a pleasing fragrance to the boy's nostrils. It was rich and sweet. Flowers and citrus.

"We'll anchor here, Birdie," the captain ordered. "Lower the rowboat and grab a bag fer fruits and medicines."

"I see the fruits on the tree limbs," Theodore said. "But where is the medicine?"

Captain Biv smiled. "In the leaves and the bark and the roots. Aurum will allow us to harvest a little."

"Where is she?" Theodore stared into the shade of the flowering green trees. A hazy mist moved through the shadows, conjuring images that did not exist. The boy's interest in the island far outweighed any reservations that might have hindered his eagerness to explore its interior and meet a maiden.

So, upon finding a foot on shore, both he and Martha entered the growth of woody greenery.

"We'll gather our fruit and medicines while yer explorin', lad," called the captain. "Greetin's to the lady fer us."

Theodore's urge to enter the trees and push forward toward the center of the small island was strong. Martha followed him faithfully, sniffing and pausing occasionally as they progressed through a tangle of trees with branches that extended to form a canopy which filtered the haze of the sun. A sandy floor was devoid of vegetation except for scattered over-ripened fruits which lay about.

Several minutes into their hike, Theodore stopped and looked up. A movement in the branches above him lured his attention. Martha had already noticed the movement and even a faint scent that went with it. She growled once and then barked as a critter poked its head down from a cluster of leaves.

"Wait, Martha." Theodore saw the head of the creature above him and quieted the Lab.

"Hello there," he said as he reached his hand up toward the furry head of the thing with big, dark eyes and floppy ears. There were tufts of green and orange feathers protruding from the top of its head. The critter's upside-down face was comical and not threatening in the least. But as soon as Theodore's fingers touched the tip of a head feather, the thing retreated its head, squealed like a field mouse and shook the tops of the tree branches in its haste toward the center of the island.

Martha was certain it was not alone. Suddenly a cry for help caused Theodore to look closer into the interior and there, past fruity trees and dunes of sand, he saw what looked to be a clearing. As he approached it, the boy found a dwelling of the most intriguing design. It was built of woven bark and sticks and domed with a leafy roof. There were no dressings on the windows and no hinges on which to hang a door at the entrance to the dwelling. A smooth, sandy area serving as a yard surrounded the tidy structure. The sound of gurgling water led the boy and the dog to the rear of the dwelling, and another plea for help drew their attention to a small porch shaded by flowering greenery. A bowl of citrus fruit placed in the center of a carved wooden table was where the beginning of a trail of orange peelings went from the table to a well formed of shells and pebbles. Sitting upon the ledge of the well was the creature Theodore had seen in the leafy cluster. Martha growled but soon was calmed and even intrigued by the creature's cooing sound.

Theodore approached it cautiously. He could see now that it was the size of a small raccoon and covered in a reddish coat of the finest fur he had ever seen. Its feet and hands resembled those of a monkey, its face like a flying squirrel, and its tail, like a lion tamer's whip that coiled up its back. When finally Theodore stood near the critter, it cooed softly and looked down into the well. An echoing whisper coaxed Theodore to peak over into the well.

"My goodness," said the boy. "I believe there is someone at the end of this rope." He touched the rope that hung from a crossbeam beneath the small roof that covered the well. Tugging the rope, he could feel the tension on it. "Helloooo," he called. He could hear the gurgle of water, and cupping his eyes, see a splash of reflection below. But there was something obstructing his view. "Is there someone down there?" he called, turning his head to the side to listen.

The critter cooed and reached out and touched Theodore's face with the tip of its cool finger. It dropped an orange peel into the well in its effort to show the boy what had happened.

Theodore searched into the big, dark eyes of the critter and finally was able to hear its thoughts. *"I cannot raise my lady from the well,"* the critter thought while extending its whip-like tail up and over the rope beam. Suddenly it left the end of the well and swung out to the center of the orifice. Upside down, it continued its thoughts. *"My lady dropped her necklace into the well and thought to retrieve it by sitting on the well bucket and having me lower her where she could possibly dive to the bottom and locate the sparkling jewel."*

"And so you were able to lower her down there?" Theodore asked.

"Well, not exactly," thought the critter. *"You see, my strength, although considered great among my kind, is not sufficient for such a chore, and I am afraid she crashed into the water while sitting on the bucket, and now lacks the strength to climb up the rope, which I am sure is wet and slick."*

Theodore walked around to the end of the beam and put both hands on the turn crank. Then, with all his might, he began turning the handle of the crank like a spinning reel. Slowly the rope wound around the beam as the boy struggled. Inch by inch and foot by foot, until finally the wet crown of the maiden of the Island of the Rue appeared. Thankfully, she was petite, and her posterior fit well within the water bucket in which she rode. She placed her hands on the well's edge and pulled herself out of the bucket. And when she stood, barefoot and dripping beside the boy who had saved her, he noticed for the first time that she was naked and obviously not ashamed of it.

"Here." Theodore broke a leaf from a tree branch that hung low near the well roof and offered it to the maiden.

"Thank you," she responded while taking the small leaf and handing it to the critter, who was still hanging upside down over the well opening. "You're a kind boy to save me from such a foolish dilemma." She turned and walked toward the porch. "Come and sit while I dress."

Theodore watched the maiden walk across the sandy yard and enter the dwelling. Then he and Martha followed and waited at the porch table.

"My name is Aurum," the maiden said as she reappeared at the back door, clothed in a thin shift gathered at the waist. The open collar of the garment allowed the boy to see the dangling necklace she brought up with her at the well.

"I'm glad you were able to retrieve your necklace," he said. "Oh! I'm Theodore Clatterbuck," the boy added as he studied a string of pearls unlike any he had ever seen or imagined. There was one for each color of the rainbow seas. Six pearls on a necklace woven from the maiden's auburn hair.

"A pearl rainbow necklace," the boy commented.

"Yes," the maiden answered, touching the pearls with her delicate fingers. Her face was saddened.

"But where is the one from the sea that surrounds you?" Theodore was puzzled.

"Oh, it would take a clever diver to retrieve that one, for it rests in the cove on the ledge of a rimcat's lair."

"What's a rimcat?" Theodore's eyes were wide.

The maiden sat down at the porch table and said, "A rimcat is a fish with the teeth of a lion and fins like razors. It's as long as you are tall and as fast as a tacker's tail whip."

Theodore raised his brow. "What's a tacker?" he asked.

Aurum shifted her eyes to the critter that sat hunched on the porch table, peeling an orange with teeth and fingers.

"Oh." The boy understood. "Tell me about this pearl. Did you lose it?"

"I was swimming in the cove one day when my necklace came unfastened, and the red and golden pearls fell off. I was able to grab the others before they were lost. I dove quickly and was able to reach out and fetch the red one, but the orange pearl fell upon the ledge of the rimcat's lair. I approached it several times, but the rimcat was not about to let me touch it, for it is fond of shiny things that are lost. Not willing to tempt its protective nature, I abandoned my efforts and left it there to sparkle from the shadow of its lair."

"Has anyone tried to help you get it back?" Theodore posed his question while conjuring up a plan.

Aurum shook her head slowly, "Oh, it would take a very creative person to devise a plan to get the pearl back."

Theodore looked at Martha. "Remember that catfish I caught under the iron bridge last year, Martha? You know, the one my dad said was impossible to fool?"

"*Yes,*" the Lab thought, "*but it didn't have teeth like a lion or fins like razors.*"

The boy smiled and turned back to Aurum. "How deep is the lair?" he asked.

"It is not very deep at all; however, if one goes out

76

too far, he will fall from the rainbow into the sky below. But the rimcat's lair is at the edge of the beach, where the sand extends out to perhaps the length of Captain Biv's schooner. Only the rimcat is brave enough to go beyond that point."

"I'll get your pearl back, Aurum," Theodore said with assurance. "I will do it. But I'll need the tacker here to help me."

The maiden looked at her strange little friend. "His name is Weymus, but..."

Theodore stopped the maiden. "Well, if his tail whip is as strong as it looks, I think we can do it."

"You are a good person to try and help me, Theodore. But it is a dangerous endeavor you are about to begin."

Theodore stood up and smiled. "What is a rainbow necklace without its colors? Or a maiden without her smile?"

"Yes." Aurum lowered her tearful eyes. "I am afraid that without the pearl, my happiness is not complete. That is the reason I went into the well today, to retrieve the necklace, for without the colors of the rainbow about my neck, I would fade from the Island of the Rue. There is no other place for me within the realm of the rainbow."

Theodore felt compassion for the maiden. "Come soon to the beach and bring Weymus with you. Then I will tell you my plan."

Aurum smiled. "We will come."

On the trek back to the cove, Martha thought, *"What is your plan, Theodore?"*

"I'm working on it, Martha. Just give me a little time."

Captain Biv was humming a little tune and puffing on his pipe when Theodore stepped out of the Rue forest. "Well, thar ye are, lad!" the captain called from the small dune on which he sat. "Me and Birdie was 'bout to give ye up fer lost."

Birdie Wiggins reeled in the line from his fishing pole and met the boy and Martha at the captain's dune. "We was fixin' to come in after ye, once the Cap'n thar finished his pipe."

Theodore was excited to see the men and wasted no time in relating the story of the maiden and her lost pearl.

The captain and Birdie listened intently and when the boy was finished, they paused in reflection, staring first at the boy and then at each other.

"Well?" Theodore finally asked. "What do you think?" He had exposed his plan to fetch the pearl from the rimcat's lair but needed the help of the captain and his first mate if it were to succeed.

"I tussled with a rimcat once and nearly lost me hand to it," Birdie said, his face hardened as he recalled the incident. "Me and the Cap'n was havin' a leisurely row 'round the other side of the island, when I happened to drop me cup of sparkling dew in about three foot o' water. That cup was give to me by a mullpuck's uncle, what was the mayor o' the township o' Clarity, in the yeller sea."

Theodore scratched his head in confusion and looked at the captain.

Captain Biv pulled the pipestem from his teeth and nodded his head. "Clarity is a town that floats upon the yeller sea. Mullpucks is the little winged creatures that live thar. The mayor is a tall and skinny feller, who deceased during a dream o' the place and stayed thar. All them little mullpucks thinks he's thar uncle."

Theodore grimaced and looked back at Birdie, who continued his story.

"Well, anyways, we stopped rowin' the boat when me cup fell o'er the side, and I reached down fer it 'bout the time a rimcat decided to claim it fer itself. It locked onto the cup's shiny trigger handle with its teeth as I grabbed the rim of the cup with me fingers." Birdie burst out laughing as he recalled the event. "That rimcat pulled so hard I flew out the boat and was dragged in the surf a ways a'fore it went fer the deep water. That's when I give that cup a powerful yank with all me might and jerked it out of that rimcat's clutch. Why I yanked it so hard that one of the rimcat's teeth came out and somehow ended up in the cup. By the time it turned 'round, I 'bout skidded on the surface o'er to the beach whar the cap'n picked me up." Birdie wiped his brow with a handkerchief. "Whew," he said while working his fingers in and out. "It still frets me to think what the teeth o' that rimcat might've done had he turned on me that day." Birdie eyeballed Theodore. "Why, now, it's the truth," he swore, "ain't it, Cap'n?" He turned his face to Captain Biv, who was now standing and putting away his pipe. The man bobbed his head in agreement.

"'Tis a true story, lad. A rimcat ain't yer typical fish, and if yer thinkin' to retrieve a bauble its taken a likin' to, well, ye best be quicker than it in yer attempt." The captain parted his legs and folded his arms across his chest. "So, what's yer plan?"

Theodore looked at the two men and without a blink of his eyes, stated the plan he had concocted on his jaunt through the Rue forest. "I'm going to tie something shiny to the end of Weymus's tail and have him taunt that rimcat with it while I swim up from behind and await my chance to grab the pearl at the edge of its lair."

The captain looked at Birdie, then back at Theodore. "Kin ye hold yer breath, lad?" he asked. "Ye might be down thar fer a spell, while the tacker is temptin' that rimcat to take a swipe."

"I can," Theodore answered without pause.

"You are not a good swimmer, Theodore," thought Martha. *"Remember the time Becky had to pull you in from the eddy below the iron bridge?"* The Lab panted her concern.

"I can swim better under the surface than on top of it," the boy countered. "And besides," he looked at the big gold earring that hung from Birdie's earlobe, "Can that rimcat avoid a chance to snag such a big, shiny bauble as that?"

The captain laughed out loud while Birdie tugged possessively at the ring in his ear. "Ye know, lad," he chuckled, "yer plan is so simple, it jest might work."

Birdie added, "Jest be hopeful the rimcat don't turn on ye when it see's what yer up to." The first mate fiddled with the earring until it came unclasped, and he held it out to Theodore.

A grunt from the edge of the Rue forest was followed by the appearance of Weymus, the tacker, who was followed closely by Aurum.

The captain and Birdie bowed respectfully as the maiden of Rue Island approached them.

"Captain Biv," she greeted the captain with a nod of her head. "Mr. Wiggins." The hint of a smile was on her lips but not the one the two men were accustomed to in their prior encounters with the woman.

Weymus whined, and Aurum bent down and brought the tacker into her arms. His affection for her was evident as he snuggled to her breasts in the cup of her arms.

"The lad has a plan to gain yer pearl, Ma'am." Captain Biv placed his hat, which he had removed at the sight of the maiden, back on his head.

"What is your plan, Theodore?" she inquired.

For a moment after the boy repeated his scheme for the maiden, she was quiet, as if contemplating the chances of his success. Finally she raised one of Weymus's floppy ears and whispered to him. When she finished, the tacker excitedly came out of her arms and climbed onto her shoulder. He turned around and in the blink of an eye, sprang his lengthy tail out in the direction of Birdie. Before the man knew it, the earring was out of his hand and in the possession of the tacker.

Theodore laughed at the astounded look on Birdie's face. "I think more than before that we have a good chance at this," the boy said.

"Whar's the rimcat's lair, Aurum?" asked the first mate.

Aurum walked to the edge of the water and pointed. "Out there," she answered. "The length of your ship and at a depth to match Theodore's height."

"I'll wade out and locate it." Theodore removed his shoes while he spoke. "Captain Biv, you and Birdie row out beyond the point I designate and have Weymus with you."

"I'll carry Weymus," Aurum insisted. "He will do best from the comfort of my arms."

"Then come aboard the boat, Ma'am." Captain Biv and Birdie waited at the water's edge for the maiden.

"Be careful, Theodore," thought Martha. *"Please!"*

Theodore bent down and rubbed the Lab's satiny ears as they watched Birdie row the boat out. "Don't worry, Martha," he consoled her. "I will be fine and back with you soon."

Martha licked him on the cheek.

While Theodore walked out into the surf, Aurum fastened Birdie's earring to the end of Weymus's tail. By the time the shiny bauble was secure, Theodore had slapped the surface of the water. He was amazed at how clear the water was. The blurred vision he had expected was minimal as he crept slowly toward the rimcat's lair. Within seconds, he spotted the domed dwelling, which resembled a shell pile laced with reddish-orange seaweed stems. Cautiously he approached the lair, and when he was close enough, he peered over it and saw the head of the resting rimcat, its lower jaw jutting out and exposing the perfectly tipped spears that were its teeth. Theodore could not see the eyes of the sea beast but imagined them cruel and dark. If the rimcat was the length of its lair and not curled within, then he surmised it to be at least three feet long.

Beyond the ledge of the lair, the depths of the sea seemed an abyss of orange, spiked by shards of light that emanated from far below.

Slowly the boy retreated from the ledge. He signaled with his hand for Birdie to row toward him quietly. When the rowboat was in position, Theodore gave the okay signal with his hand and sank below the surface. By the time he was back at the rimcat's lair, Birdie had brought the rowboat in close enough so that Weymus could lower his tail with the lure to where the sea beast could see it.

Now the nature of a rimcat is such that even the slightest movement of anything that comes within the perimeters of its sight and looks edible in the least will awaken a predatory instinct many times that of most game fish we know of on earth. It is a fact, however, that rimcats do not require much sustenance, as they live in vapor-made seas that form and then reform. But a shiny bobble or even a sparkling ripple upon the surface of the sea will ignite an instant and violent response from this otherwise dormant ledge dweller. That being said, as soon as the rimcat saw that shiny earring dangling at the end of Weymus's tail, its desire to possess it became its only reason to live.

Theodore peeked over the dome of the creature's lair and waited for it to dart out after the lure. It was a good thing the clarity of the water was such that all in the boat, especially Weymus, could see clearly to the depth of the lair, for just as the rimcat bolted for the earring, Weymus yanked his tail with such force that the sea creature broke the surface of the water and flew up over the boat in its pursuit. The tacker coiled his tail in tight, as everybody except Birdie ducked their heads. The rimcat could have made a high arch over the rowboat and back into the cove if its flight path was clear, but the first mate of the *Wind Sailor* had his own design concerning the sea beast.

"Got ye!" cried Birdie as he launched a harpoon into the sharp tail of the rimcat.

Captain Biv held his cap down on his head with one hand as he grabbed at Birdie's leg with the other, lest the first mate leave the rowboat with his prize.

"Let go, Birdie!" the captain cried out, losing his grip.

Birdie Wiggins sprung into the air behind the wriggling tail fin of the largest rimcat anyone had ever seen. He let go just as the tacker's tail quickly shot out and wrapped around the beast and hurled it so far out to sea that it would be a long while before the rimcat found its way back to its lair.

"Thank ye," Birdie said to Weymus as he lay breathless in the boat. "I don't know what got into me."

The captain patted his first mate on the shoulder. "It's best ye lost it, Birdie, or else we might'a lost ye."

The rowboat was still rocking in the water when Aurum pointed to shore. "Look! Theodore got the orange pearl!"

The boy's snatch of the pearl was quick and precise,

and as he stood on the beach marveling at its beauty, he was very proud of himself.

"I'll never forget your cunning and courage, Theodore Clatterbuck," Aurum spoke as she threaded the pearl back onto her necklace. "Here," she offered the necklace to Theodore and turned so that he could fasten it around her delicate neck. "Thank you," she said when he finished. A big smile formed on her lips as she touched the pearl and turned around. Her face was aglow with happiness, and a rainbow aura emanated from her body. "All for a maiden's smile," Theodore said softly.

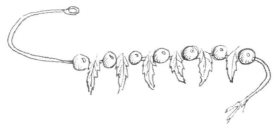

Aurum touched the boy on the shoulder. "You will go far, Theodore, for the courage you possess is touched by a caring heart."

Theodore raised his shoulders and stood a little taller. He looked into the eyes of the maiden and then over at Captain Biv and Birdie. "Well, I guess we are off to another adventure, then?" He raised his eyebrows.

"Ye kin bet on it, lad," the captain chuckled. He bowed to Aurum. "Hold to them pearls, Ma'am, fer yer not likely ta know the likes o' this one ag'in."

The maiden of the Rue Island smiled and nodded.

Theodore was amazed at how the sunlight shone

through the depths of the sea as the maiden smiled, then turned back to the interior of the island. Weymus jumped up onto her shoulder when she entered the drifting mist that dampened the leaves of the trees. The tacker looked back and thought, *"Goodbye, brave boy."*

Theodore looked down and patted Martha on the head. "Where to next, Captain?" he called out as he watched Captain Biv and Birdie readying the rowboat for the gentle surf and the short trip out to the *Wind Sailor*. He and Martha climbed into the boat when the bow was pointed out to sea, and Birdie waited to push them off.

"We're 'bout to come onto the yeller sea, lad," said the captain. "Thar's brighter sunshine, and a town what floats on the water, like a cloud in the sky. Ye'll not believe it 'til ye see it."

"Let's go." Theodore picked up the oar handles, set the blades and pushed forward, while Birdie nudged them into the surf and jumped into the boat. "Yer doin' fine, lad," said the first mate. Birdie winked at the captain and lit his pipe. "I always like sailin' the yeller sea and visitin' Clarity. But fer an eyeful o' beauty, they don't come more fetchin' than the little maiden we just left in the Rue."

Theodore heard Birdie's comment but did not answer. Instead he rowed the boat steadily toward the schooner, with a vision of Becky Bloom in his mind. There was none fairer than she to him. Not even the maiden of the Rue Island.

The Yellow Sea

AROUND THE RUE ISLAND and out to sea, the *Wind Sailor* sped, its sails full in the wind.

"We've entered the Yeller Sea, lad," said Captain Biv.

Theodore noticed the sails had become the color of the sea. He watched the captain steer the schooner while he stood at the starboard and listened as the old sailor spoke. "It won't be long now 'til we see Clarity a'floatin' like a cloud."

"But how do you know where to steer the schooner?" Theodore had noticed the lack of navigation instruments near the helm and could not help but wonder how the captain knew his bearings, for there was only daylight in the realm of the rainbow. "The sunlight is deflected everywhere and here, seems to be coming up from the depths of the sea." The boy was confused.

The captain smiled. "'Tis the moisture that's always in the air that deflects the light in a rainbow, lad. But the main burst of light always comes from the west. When ye sail the seas of the rainbow as much as me, ye git real good at readin' the signs that's all 'round ye. Wind an' waves, currents an' sun streaks."

"But how do you find this place called Clarity, Captain Biv?" Theodore searched out to sea with his hands cupped over his eyes. "All I see is water and a yellow haze in the sky."

"Look beyond the jib sail, lad," the captain replied. "In the sky, thar ahead of us." Captain Biv tipped his head in the direction he spoke of. "Watch fer a minute, through the haze, and ye'll see a little black dot movin' steadily, just above the horizon."

Theodore searched until suddenly he called out, "I see one! No, two. No. I see lots of them. What are they?"

Captain Biv smiled. "Mullpucks. They don't stray out far from the floating town. Not far a'tall. So when you see 'em, ye foller 'em, and by the time I finish this bowl of tobacca in me pipe, we'll be thar."

Theodore squinted his eyes at the black dots soaring in the distance. "What in the world is a mullpuck, Captain?" he asked.

The captain chuckled and leaned back in his chair. "Why, tis a bird what resembles a penguin on earth, 'cept fer a long tuft of hair that tops its crown like a feather duster and a hooked beak what sports the colors of the rainbow. Its big beady eyes is rimmed with curly blond feathers, and its fin-like tail acts as a rudder in the air or in the water. It whimpers like a monkey and chatters like a squirrel. It's got no use fer a nest like any bird you ever seen."

Theodore walked across the deck and leaned against the gunnel. "Sailing the rainbow seas is a peculiar adventure, Captain," the boy said. "You never know what to expect."

The captain grinned. "Sech is life, lad. And that's

why it's best to be prepared fer what ye least expect."

The *Wind Sailor* came upon the township of Clarity just as Captain Biv said it would. As he finished his pipe and was tucking it in his vest pocket, he brought the schooner portside to a narrow dock.

Mullpucks were everywhere in the sky and water. The small ones were playful with one another, and the larger ones were attentive and orderly. They aligned the dock and left way for a footpath that led to the outskirts of the town.

Now one might wonder about the appearance of a town inhabited solely, except for one human, by mullpucks. Within the realm of a rainbow, things are possible that one can barely conceive of in the outer realms. A mere dream on earth can be a reality there.

Not so long ago, a man by the name of Spiley Rigor, spent most of his life on earth on the main stage of his mind, with an imaginary audience. You see, he spoke to himself as one who is entertaining a crowd with tales. But there was no one in Spiley's audience. His stories were of a strange nature. They were short and erratic. There was no clarity to his thoughts, no order. His memory was such that he would begin with the ending of a story and finish with its beginning. This mental instability also made it impossible for Spiley to obtain and hold a job. No woman would have him either, and for the most part, he was avoided and even shunned by people in general. Even so, he loved to tell his stories. So he continued and found that the only audience he could hold were the birds and animals that saw no harm in him. So he lived on the outskirts of a town on earth and walked the fields and forests where he was accepted for who he was. Also given to dreams, Spiley Rigor could conjure up the most vivid imaginings. In a daydream, he once saw a giant groundhog hollow out the earth beneath the town in which he was born until it was as thin as a sheet of ice on a pond. Fearing it would collapse, he ran into the town screaming an alarm until, for his sake and sanity and the nerves of those hearing his cries, the local authorities locked him away. This sort of thing happened so often that the local jail had a special cell for Spiley, with cushioned walls and a mat on the floor. It was in this cell when he was very old that Spiley had a dream of a great and beautiful rainbow he had seen one day while talking with his animal friends. In his dream, Spiley went to a yellow sea, where strange little birds floated on the surface without a home. Since in his dream he was floating in the misty air above them, he thought to imagine a place for them. And as he thought, so his thoughts became, until everything he imagined came true right there on the water. Yes, Spiley created a town with his mind and determination. A home for the strange little birds and also a place for himself. He imagined pebble streets and small huts with thatched roofs and windows with no panes. There were brightly painted stores, where cheerful merchants only appeared with the opening of the door, and cafés and restaurants where one's dietary desires appeared on a plate in front of them. The mullpucks had little interest in stores and cafés. They did, however, live in the huts like humans. They even sat in chairs and around tables and so enjoyed the strange tales of Spiley Rigor.

When Spiley had finished imagining his town within the rainbow, he sadly turned to leave, for he knew it was only a dream. But the mullpucks, who were so grateful for a home, urged him to stay, and soon his feet touched the pebble streets he had imagined and with the passing of his life on earth, his dream became a reality. The mullpucks looked upon him as a wise and good uncle. And Spiley Rigor, who had never fit in on earth, had a home forever in the realm of a rainbow.

"Come and sit with me," the tall, spindly man encouraged his guests as he reached out his hands. "I see the mullpucks have guided you back to Clarity, Captain Biv," he said with a warm smile. "It is good to see you again." Spiley shook the captain's hand and then, turning to Birdie, said, "And, Birdie, I hope you have brought more tales of your exploits on the seas to me."

Birdie grasped Spiley's hand and shook it rigorously. "A story fer a plate, Spiley. How's that?"

Spiley's laugh was infectious. "Of course. Come. We'll walk to the café and have a bite to eat."

"What's on the spit?" Birdie asked.

"Whatever you wish for, Birdie," Spiley answered, looking then at Theodore. "And who is this?" he asked.

"Theodore...Clatterbuck." The boy cleared his throat between his first and last name and reached out to shake the man's hand. "And this is Martha," he added.

"Welcome, Theodore and Martha."

The walk to midtown only took a few minutes. Theodore was amazed at the mullpucks. Their behavior was exemplary, and they accompanied the humans and Martha as one would expect a following of friends. The small whimpers they emitted with each wobbling step were comical, but the birds were agile and could take to flight without a running start.

"I haven't perceived any words in thought from the mullpucks, Mr. Rigor." Theodore was confused. The boy could hear Martha's thoughts and even those of the tacker, Weymus, on the Rue Island in the Orange Sea.

"They only funnel their thoughts toward me, Theodore," answered the man as he sat down in a chair outside the café. "I'm not sure why. They certainly could communicate if they wished to. They are highly intelligent birds and certainly capable."

"I never got a word from 'em," Birdie spoke up as he brought a thin slice of steak to his lips. "But they are of a friendly nature."

Theodore was amazed at the full plates in front of the captain and Birdie. Steaming plates of food for both men made his mouth water, and suddenly a double cheeseburger with lettuce, tomato, and mustard appeared on his, along with side orders of potato wedges and a tub of ketchup. A fizzing soda filled his empty glass. A bowl for Martha went from empty to full of warm gravy and beef chunks. Theodore raised his eyebrow at the Lab. "Martha, you only get dry food."

Martha looked at Theodore and then down at the

bowl of food. *"This doesn't happen every day, Theodore. Can we just go with it, please?"*

The boy smiled. "Go ahead, girl. Enjoy."

The captain chuckled as he watched the Lab greedily devour her meal.

When all had eaten, Spiley rose from his chair and said, "I will ask Theodore and Martha to walk with me, if you don't mind, Captain, Birdie."

The captain nodded his approval and looked over at Birdie, who had just imagined a big piece of fudge pie on his plate, complete with whipped cream and a cherry.

"We're fine here, Spiley. Really, we are," the captain said while breaking apart a large chocolate chip cookie.

Theodore rose from his chair and joined the tall man. Martha stepped close to his side, and the three walked for several blocks.

"I want to show you something, Theodore," Spiley said pointing to a spiraling staircase that stood apart from any other structure and led up to a very high crow's nest, which obviously served as a lookout point.

The boy and dog followed Spiley up the winding steps until finally they stood atop the floating township.

"Wow!" Theodore said. "I can see everything so clearly from up here." He pointed. "Across the Yellow Sea and back to the Island of the Rue and beyond that, to the Red Sea." There was excitement in the boy's voice. "Look, Martha. There's the silhouette of Split Nose Mary's ship." He looked at Spiley Rigor and then down at the town of Clarity. "You've built a beautiful place here, Mr. Rigor."

Spiley smiled. "My life below the rainbow was without order. My thoughts, inconsistent and confused. I was perceived as someone I was not. But in my heart, I knew my nature. I begged men to listen to me, but they could not see past the wildness in my dress or hear past the ranting of my mind. Only the animals and the birds would hear me. And for that, I was thankful, for at least among them I was not judged. This is the dream I aspired to, where there is orderliness and no confusion. I named the town Clarity because it represents the clearness of thought that I was unable to find on earth. I live in a rainbow, Theodore. It is a place where a dream can come true. I stayed because I had given up on earth. But you do not have to stay. For you, the lessons are here that will show you that you need not dwell here to see your dreams come true."

Tears blurred Theodore's vision as he looked out over the colorful seas and listened to Spiley. Martha could sense his sadness and leaned her muzzle against his leg.

"It's hard for me down there," the boy finally admitted. "I'm seen as a fool and treated badly. The kids at school laugh at me because I'm clumsy, or they hate me for the grades I make. They call me poor and think I'm pathetic."

Spiley Rigor knew this young man better than Theodore could have imagined. It was his job to know him, because only certain individuals can exist within the realms of a rainbow. They are chosen with exquisite care and placed there according to their gifts.

Spiley was a wise man with a heart as big as the sea he lived upon. "What is the beauty of the mullpucks, Theodore?" the man finally asked. "And of your companion, Martha?" He reached down and touched the Lab's head. "What is it that allows them to live each day seemingly without worry or stress? Think."

Theodore was silent in his thoughts until a word finally slipped through his lips. "Freedom," he whispered at first. "Freedom," he then repeated aloud.

Spiley smiled. "Yes," he responded. "From the time they open their eyes, they allow life to wrap itself around them. They do not fear the future or dwell in the past. Lessons are stored, shaping their natures. They are inquisitive, bright and intuitive. They are loyal to a fault. But perhaps, most of all, they are forgiving, for even after the harshest reprimands or the hours of neglect, they are there to be the friends we need. Their fondness for us is unconditional. Their patience is indelible. Perhaps their minds see the goodness in us that we should see in our fellow man. They can somehow see through the cloak of issues we wear and the shades of stress that darken our spirits at times."

Theodore bent down and stroked Martha's satiny ears with his hand. "You are right, Mr. Rigor," he said. "Animals are easy. But sometimes it's hard to see through the badness in people."

Spiley nodded his head once. "Yes, and in difficult situations with people, insight will bring about clarity. Listen to their words and observe their actions carefully. Therein lies the pathway to understanding them and reaching out to them as no other person has before."

Spiley put his hand on Theodore's shoulder. "Try this toward the ones who persecute you, and you will see that in most instances, there is goodness in all."

A flock of mullpucks flew in from the western sky and circled over their heads as Spiley led Theodore and Martha back down the winding stairs and onto the pebble street. Theodore watched the strange little birds as they separated and went to their respective homes along the corridors of the town. The narrow streets abounded with the hustle and bustle of the wobbling creatures. They seemed to Theodore like humans in a way, in that they walked about chattering and visiting with each other.

"Why do these birds look to you as their uncle, when you are not even of their own kind?" Theodore asked.

Spiley raised his hand, and a mullpuck flew up from the street and perched on his forearm. "Because they allow themselves the ability to look past the outside to see what is within," he answered while offering a seed to the bird. The mullpuck took the seed and flew up to the rooftop of a small row house. "Remember this, Theodore." Spiley stopped walking and turned to the boy. "No man is anything unless his heart speaks it. Only then will others know him for what he is."

Spiley Rigor was a wise man, and as the *Wind Sailor* pulled away from the dock outside the town of Clarity later that day, Theodore thought a lot about what he had said. He thought about freedom and forgiveness, about seeing through personas and into hearts.

When the floating town was a distant shape on the horizon, Theodore closed his hand around a yellow pebble he had picked up from the main street of Clarity and closed his eyes. He tried to picture in his mind the cruel face of Bently Card when he last saw him at the iron bridge. But he could not conjure up the boy's features. Instead he envisioned Bently's eyes darting back and forth from Blue to Jerry to Benny and then back to him. Now in his mind's eye, he could see what at first he mistook for cruelty. Now he realized that it was hurt that drove the boy. It was as if Theodore could see a tunnel through Bently's eyes that led straight to the boy's heart. For a moment there was compassion in Theodore's heart for his tormentor, until suddenly he opened his eyes and shook his head. A single tear streaked down his cheek as a slicing pain gripped his side. He sat down slowly on the deck and leaned back against a sail post.

Birdie's voice called from the first mate's place at the bow of the schooner, but Theodore could not answer. His heart pounded in his chest, until slowly, he was calmed by the touch of Martha, who licked his dampened cheek and nuzzled his neck.

"It's all right, Theodore." Her thought assured him. "I'm here with you. I won't leave you." Martha's thoughts echoed in Theodore's mind as he drifted to sleep beneath the full sails of the *Wind Sailor*.

The Green Sea

BETWEEN THE YELLOW AND BLUE SEAS of the rainbow is one of balance and of harmony. On the color spectrum, it is the point of color midway between red and violet. The Green Sea is where the mind and spirit merge. Humans recognize more variation in green than in any other color. We are drawn to it, for it is synonymous with the beginning of life. It is where balance is found in nature.

The sails of the *Wind Sailor* had turned as green as a Granny Smith apple when finally Theodore opened his eyes. The full weathered faces of Captain Biv and his first mate were so close when the boy focused that he was startled.

Martha eagerly lapped at his chin when he pushed up on his elbows. "Okay, girl." He smiled. "I'm okay." He pulled her to him.

"I was worried," she thought.

"Ye left us fer a bit thar, lad," Captain Biv spoke as softly as he could, but still his voice was raspy and louder than most. "We've come upon the Green Sea, as ye kin see here by the sails a'blowin'."

Theodore looked up and saw the green sails bulging with the warm breeze.

"Um." Birdie stood up. "Take ye a whiff o' that breeze, lad. Grandpa's orchard is upwind of us." The man smacked his lips. "I sure wouldn't mind me a bite of them apples, what grow thar."

Theodore smelled the air. "I do smell apples! Who is Grandpa?"

Birdie looked at the captain who shrugged his shoulders and stood up.

Captain Biv scratched his head while looking out to sea. "Well, we don't really know who Grandpa was a'fore he got here, but he did find a hill a'floatin' on the sea and decided to plant him an apple orchard on it. It didn't take long fer it to be a real sight to us, and finally, one day, we anchored and asked if we could pick some of them green apples we'd been smellin' in passin'. Well it was all right with the old man then, but as time went on, he became a bit ornery."

"Yep," Birdie chimed in. "He got to whar he wouldn't let nobody have an apple anymore. Told the captain that a troll from down below had swum up from the bottom of the Green Sea an' spat on every apple tree in his orchard."

"Spat on the trees?" Theodore could hardly believe his ears. "How did a troll, if there is such a thing, get into the Green Sea in the first place?"

"Well," the captain looked over at Birdie and took the lead on the explanation. "It seems a twister pulled him out from under a bridge and throwed him so hard up in the sky, that he broke through the bottom of the sea an' surfaced at Grandpa's orchard."

The captain looked over at Birdie, expecting him to continue the story.

Birdie obliged without a fuss. "Yep, fer sure he did,

an' then he asked ol' Grandpa fer a bite o' apple. But the ol' man won't much fer sharin' his apples by then, what made the troll real angry. So he commenced to spittin' on all them good trees, which is a troll's way o' layin' claim to somethin'."

"What happened to Grandpa?" Theodore seemed concerned.

"Well," Captain Biv started, "he floats the sea on a raft made o' applewood logs and lives off the bark o' them logs and green turtle soup. We see him occasionally, but he's in no mood to be friendly these days, what with losin' his orchard to a troll." The captain looked over at Birdie and then at Theodore. "He tol' us the last time we seen him, that if anyone was ever to git his orchard back fer him, that he'd be grateful enough to share them apples ag'in with everyone who comes along. Didn't he say that, Birdie?"

The first mate winked and stomped the deck. "He sure did, Cap'n, sure as I'm standin' here, he did."

Theodore walked over to port and leaned over the gunnel. "Where's the orchard?" he asked.

"The breeze is takin' us near it now, lad," answered the captain. "We'll be thar soon."

Theodore thought for a moment, then straightened his shoulders and turned around to face the captain and Birdie. "I'm going to get us some of those apples," he announced confidently. "And I'm going to get the old man's orchard back for him. If you can get me to that hill, I'll do it."

Martha barked, *"Not without me, you won't."* She turned a circle on the deck and stood looking up at

Theodore. *"I'm with you in this, Theodore, and if you are going up against this troll, then so am I."* The Lab was firm with her thoughts.

"Okay, girl." Theodore gave in quick. "But it might be dangerous," he warned.

"What's your plan?" Martha sat and waited. She knew there probably was not a well thought-out plan yet.

"I'll let you know when we get there," the boy replied.

Captain Biv clapped his hands and hurried back to the helm of the schooner. "Good, then. The breeze is pickin' up now. We'll be thar soon. Ye best git con-coctin' that plan, lad."

Birdie patted the boy on the shoulder. "Yer a brave one, lad. Things has been a bit out'a balance in the Green Sea ever since that troll got here. It's 'bout time someone come along and did somethin' 'bout it."

Now, Grandpa had been adrift on the Green Sea for quite a spell when he saw the *Wind Sailor* coming toward his raft. "Where are you heading, Captain?" he called.

Birdie dropped the sails enough for the schooner to slow down so the captain could answer the old man.

"We're transportin' a lad here name o' Theodore Clatterbuck, who has a mind to git yer orchard back fer ye, if'n, that is, ye agree to share some o' them delicious treats with us in return. What say ye, Grandpa?"

Grandpa was so tired of eating bark and green turtle soup by then that he would have agreed to anything. But it is true that he indeed wanted his orchard back, and he would not hesitate in sharing his apples for it. He hung his thumbs over his belt and leaned his head back. "I've been floating the sea for so long on this miserable raft that I'm more than willing to go for anything to get my feet back on land. And if I eat any more green turtle soup, I'm afraid I'll start growing a shell on my back. What's the boy's plan?"

"Well, right now, I don't have one," answered Theodore. "But by the time we get to the orchard, I will."

The old man laughed out loud. "That's good enough for me, son. Bring me aboard, Birdie."

Another quarter of a mile and the floating orchard came into clear view.

"Whar is that cuss?" Birdie asked from the bow of the anchored schooner.

"Oh, don't worry, Birdie," replied Grandpa. "Once the boy steps a foot on shore, he'll show himself. Believe me, I've been run off a few times." The old man turned to Theodore. "What's your plan, boy?"

Theodore did not hesitate in answering. "Oh, I'm going to talk to him," he said in a matter-of-fact manner.

There was silence for a minute, while the three men wrapped their brains around Theodore's plan.

"Have ye ever tried talkin' to a troll, lad?" Captain Biv asked.

"No, sir. I can't say as I have, Captain. As a matter of fact, I didn't even think they really existed until now."

"Ere ye afraid, lad?" Birdie leaned in and asked.

"Not yet." Theodore searched hard for any movement in the orchard. "I guess I'm all right." He looked down at Martha. "How are you doing, girl?"

The Lab barked, then spun around. *I'm just looking forward to getting off this boat for awhile,* she thought.

"You are a mighty brave young man, Theodore Clatterbuck." Grandpa patted the boy on the shoulder. "Good luck to you."

"Thanks," Theodore said as he slipped over the side of the schooner. The men lowered Martha down into the rowboat and watched as Theodore rowed them to shore.

The orchard in the Green Sea was the most extravagant grove of apple trees that Theodore had ever seen. The old man had planted his apple seeds well, for they were spaced perfectly and until recently, tended to with great care and expertise. Of course, now with the troll in charge of the orchard, green weeds and vines were beginning to grow and broaden their reach. The boy could tell that it would not be long before the trees would be strangled by vines and choked by weeds.

"Come on, Martha," he said as he stepped from the boat and onto the shore.

The Lab obeyed, but as soon as the boy and dog took a few steps, a thunderous voice called from the grove. "Who is this boy and mongrel that comes to my orchard for to steal my apples?" The thrashing of brush and tree branches followed the troll's roaring question.

Martha growled and lowered her head.

Theodore swallowed and answered as loud as he

could. "It is I, Theodore Clatterbuck, the fastest runner in the realm of the rainbow and my vicious guardian, Martha!"

"Really?" Martha growled between thoughts. *"I'm doing my best mean growl here."*

Suddenly a roar of disapproval shuddered through the orchard, and tree limbs were pushed and parted until the troll appeared.

"Vicious, eh?" he posed his wicked question while moving closer to the boy and his dog.

Theodore could hardly believe the size of the creature, who stood a good nine feet tall. Distorted muscles bulged on his thick body from neck to calf. His filthy fingers were short and stubby. His feet, wide and flat. His face, a contorted mass of swells and creases, his eyeballs were horse size and threatened to pop from their sockets. His brow tightened with anger as he spoke. "I've eaten morsels from muscle shells bigger than the two of you," he scoffed. "Vicious," he repeated with a smirk and an eyeball on Martha. "I've seen more threat from a crawdad." He threw his head back and laughed wickedly before glaring at Theodore. "Now tell me, boy, how is the fastest runner in the realm of the rainbow going to avoid the doom you've brought on yourself and your mongrel for coming onto my orchard, eh? Tell me." The troll folded his massive arms across his swelled chest and waited for Theodore's response.

Theodore cleared his throat. "Well, sir, I'm going to run to the top of the hill there, where the biggest of your apples grow and collect enough for me and my friends out there on that schooner. We are going to eat them and save the seeds so that Grandpa can start another orchard, bigger and better than the one you stole from him."

A wicked grin stretched across the troll's leathery lips. "Well, then let's just see you get past me." He crouched and readied himself for Theodore's attempt.

The boy forced a chuckle. Then in a serious tone, spiced up his challenge. "I'd be willing to wager that I can fill this bag I brought," he reached into the bow of the rowboat and withdrew a canvas sack he had placed there while still on the *Wind Sailor*, "with enough apples for Grandpa to start several orchards."

"And I would say you'd lose that wager, if you had anything to offer." The troll's fury was turning into intrigue. "I have an apple orchard, but what have you got that I would want?"

Theodore thought quick. He slapped the side of the rowboat with the canvas sack and kicked it with his shoe. "This rowboat could be yours to float around your orchard, if I lose."

The troll laughed out loud. "Yes, and I can watch you work my trees while I feast on the ribs of that mongrel of yours."

Martha growled and then looked up at Theodore. *"Okay, I'm ready to go back to the schooner now,"* she thought. *"Really, Theodore, do you have a real plan here?"*

Theodore looked at Martha and whispered, "It's coming, don't worry."

There was game in the troll's threat, and Theodore

picked up on it. "What about this, troll?" he conjured. "If I make it to the top of the hill and get back to my boat with the bag full of apples, then you give the orchard back to the old man and move on to another place. But if I lose, then you get the rowboat, and I'll work the orchard for you."

"And what about the mongrel?" The troll rubbed his bulging chin with his fingers and licked his lips. His overconfidence was fueled with greed. "Instead of eating it, I might just need a pet to help me bide my leisure time."

The Lab growled as the hair raised along her back.

"Fair enough," Theodore agreed. "Now let me explain our wager to Martha so that she will know to honor it if I lose."

The troll laughed. "You do that, boy," he called, "and tell it that if it is a good pet, I won't eat it."

Theodore bent down on one knee and brought the Lab close to him. "Now when it starts, you run interference for me, girl. Make the troll pause and stumble, or there is no way I can outrun him. His stride is too great, and you know I'm not that fast a runner. I've noticed that one of his legs is shorter than the other, so keep that in mind coming down the hill, if we get that far. Can you do it, girl?" Theodore looked into the eyes of the Lab, his hands behind her ears in a firm caress.

Martha looked at the ugly troll and then back at Theodore. *I'll run circles around that giant slug. Just you make it back to the boat,* she thought.

Theodore smiled and rubbed her satiny ears. "I will, Martha, I promise."

"Make your move, boy!" the troll roared. He stomped his feet and readied himself.

Tense seconds passed before Theodore sprang into action, heading for the trees a dozen paces from the edge of the water. In two strides, the troll was about to grab the boy, when Martha shot between his legs and nipped him on the inside of his ankle. The troll yelled and stumbled as Theodore entered among the apple trees. He could hear the thrashing of leaves and the breaking of limbs as the troll regained his footing and charged from behind.

Fearing the troll's gain on the boy, Martha began zigzagging back and forth in front of the troll, bringing confusion to his footing. Once he tripped and then rolled back into his gait, and once he crashed into a tree trunk, which did temporarily stop him. Angry and determined, the troll continued his pursuit of the boy, who had by then gained access to the top of the hill and was pulling and stuffing apples into the open sack.

The troll was furious. Never would he have imagined with his gloating self-assurance that a mere boy could better him. An instant fear of losing touched a place inside him that he had refused to think of for a long time. It was a memory, a distant cloud of coherence that brought tears to his eyes and slowed him until finally he stopped and slumped to the ground, his head against a tree trunk.

Martha stopped when the troll did and waited silently and cautiously.

When Theodore saw what had happened, he finished filling his sack with apples and carefully approached the troll.

Martha sensed the troll's depression as she stood panting nearby. Her ability to perceive humanistic traits was not blocked by his facade of wickedness and cruelty. Not once had she believed that he would do real harm to Theodore, or that he would carry out his threat to eat her. There was something sad and protective in his abrasive threats. Something she could detect with her ultra senses.

By the time Theodore walked to the trail, Martha was already sitting calmly beside the troll and allowing his fingers to touch her paw. *"He is not wicked,"* she thought, looking up at Theodore. *"He is sad and tired."*

Theodore laid his sack of apples down and knelt close to the troll. He could hear the raspy breathing as the troll's chest heaved from the exertion of the chase.

Martha nuzzled the troll's shoulder in a kind gesture. Slowly the troll raised his head and looked at the Lab. A faint smile crossed his lips, and he gently patted her on the shoulder. Then he turned his attention to Theodore.

"I am not a troll," he quietly admitted with tears filling his eyes.

Theodore sat down and waited patiently. He could tell the creature wanted to explain. "Take your time," the boy responded sympathetically. "I am also not the fastest runner within the realm of the rainbow. And…" He reached over and touched Martha on her head. "Martha is not vicious at all."

The creature rubbed his moistened eyes and straightened his posture as best he could. "My name is Resin Cane, a name my drunken daddy no doubt took great humor in giving me when he first laid his eyes on my distorted body. My mother gave me nothing but love as long as she lived, but I lost her to a bad heart when I was young and was forced to live under my daddy's cruel and drunken influence until a tree fell through the roof one night and crushed him in his sleep. Having no relations that wanted me or friends to turn to, I was forced to live off the land and fend for myself. That is how I came to live under the bridge on the edge of a town I knew as a boy. That is when they began to refer to me as "the troll." My real name was lost. When the twister landed me here, I found the most beauty I had ever seen in this orchard. But when the old man was reluctant to accept me, I became the thing the world below wanted me to be, a troll. I shouted and roared and threatened, until the old man built a raft and left his orchard." The sad man looked into Theodore's eyes. "Do you know what it is to be shunned and ridiculed, boy? To feel alone? Judged for things you cannot change?"

Theodore's compassion for the man grew with each word of his story. And he understood more than Resin Cane could have known. He reached out and touched the man's shoulder. No longer did he see him as a troll, a distorted and vile creature, but as a man dealt an abnormal body at birth, who was reaching out for help. The truth was that Theodore could see himself in Resin Cane.

"My name is Theodore Clatterbuck," he started, "and yes, I know what it is like to be shunned and ridiculed. I am not alone, for there are those who care for me, but I have known the loneliness you must feel, and I have learned to use it for the betterment of myself and the basis for the dream I have."

"But look at me, Theodore." Resin had no doubt given in to the public's perception of what he was and who he could be. "If I look the part of a troll, then how can I change that or dream beyond it?"

Theodore knew Resin's struggle. It was his, also. But his life was changing, evolving into what he knew it could be. There was hope now that he had not seen before. If he could only get back home. He could make it happen. He knew he could. He could do most anything, if he set his mind to it. Had he not saved Martha from Split Nose Mary and her motley crew of headless swordsmen? He had saved the maiden of the Rue Island by raising her from the well, and then by facing the rimcat, he retrieved her shiny pearl. He thought of the wisdom of Spiley Rigor and reached into his pocket and brought out the yellow pebble he had picked up from the main street of Clarity.

"Look at this, Resin," he offered the pebble to the man.

"What is it?" Resin held the beautiful pebble between his forefinger and thumb and examined it carefully.

"It came from a town called Clarity, and it is a reminder to me that to understand and respect myself is the stepping stone of what makes dreams come true. I might not be what others think I should be, but I know inside what I can be."

Resin smiled and handed the pebble back to Theodore. "You are a wise young man, Theodore Clatterbuck."

Theodore put the pebble back into his pocket. "I'm getting there," he said as if reassuring himself. He stood up and picked up his sack of apples.

Resin patted Martha on her head and then slowly stood up. "I'm sorry for coming on the way I did, Theodore." Resin reached out his hand and was happy that Theodore did not hesitate to grasp it firmly. He looked down at Martha. "I would not have harmed you either, Martha. If I had had a companion as faithful as you in the world below, perhaps it would have made a difference." He touched the Lab's nose with his fingers in a show of kindness.

"What do you want, Resin?" Theodore asked as they walked among the apple trees toward the shore. "Do you want to stay here or go back with me to the earth below?"

"If the old man will have me, I'd like to stay and help him in the orchard. This is a good place to find oneself, and as you say, gain some self-respect. Perhaps one day, I will go aboard that schooner you came on and follow you back."

By the time they had reached the shore, Grandpa was waiting beside his applewood raft, which he had pulled alongside the rowboat. He was surprised to see the troll with Theodore and Martha.

"I figured you had either whipped him or he'd

eaten the both of you," the old man said. "Things sure did get mighty quiet after a lot of roaring and crashing." The old man looked at the boy and then at Resin. "So what's it gonna be, troll? Are you leaving or what?"

Resin looked at Theodore and grinned. Then he turned his attention to the old man. "I'll stay, if you'll have me, Grandpa. I'm strong and can work hard. And I'd like to learn what you can teach about growing apple trees and caring for them."

The old man tugged at his earlobe and grinned. "I guess I can keep you on, troll," he responded. "But there's going to be some changes."

"Resin is my name, Grandpa." Resin approached the old man and offered his hand. "And I'm not really a troll."

Grandpa shook Resin's hand. "You got a last name?" he asked.

"Never mind that," Resin chuckled. "I think the two of us are going to have a long and bountiful relationship from now on." He winked a big eye at Theodore and Martha as he and the old man walked into the misty shadows of the apple trees.

"Thank you, Theodore," the old man called as they disappeared. "You all enjoy those apples and come back to see me and Resin anytime. And tell Captain Biv and Birdie they are always welcome here!"

Later, back on the *Wind Sailor*, Birdie hoisted the sails while Theodore raised the anchor. "Ye done good back thar, lad," Birdie spoke as he cut a green apple into slices with his jackknife. He plopped a piece into his mouth and offered one to Theodore. "I don't know what ye said, but the end result was right as can be."

Theodore chewed his slice of apple and walked back to the helm of the schooner where Martha was sitting, contented beside the captain.

"How does that apple taste, lad?" Captain Biv asked while turning the ship's steering wheel away from the orchard.

"Sweet, Captain," the boy answered. "Mighty sweet."

The Blue Sea

If the Green Sea seemed vast to Theodore, then the transition into the Blue Sea, although it was without challenges and devoid of any scale of known time to the boy, brought him and Martha and the crew of the *Wind Sailor* onto an infinite seascape.

The wind that filled the now blue sails of the schooner was a gentle and steady one.

"At the top of the rainbow is the Red Sea," the boy wondered out loud while leaning against a gunnel close to where the captain stood at the wheel of the *Wind Sailor.* "Then why have I not felt the fall into what is now obviously a blue sea?"

Captain Biv smiled and allowed a wisp of pipe smoke to lift from his breath as he answered. "The realm of a rainbow is not anythin' like the earth below it or the sky above, lad. To come into it is to enter a place whar yer willin' to accept a reality which cannot be seen or felt by another or even imagined by most. When up is down and down is up, then everythin' in between seems level."

Theodore turned around and faced the captain. "But this is real, isn't it?" he questioned. "I mean, you are here and there is Birdie, and even Martha has come here with me."

Captain Biv smiled and nodded his head. "Yes, lad.

Me and Birdie are here fer ye. And Martha is here by yer side, because thar is none as faithful or loyal to ye as she who has chosen to enter this realm of the rainbow with ye."

Theodore looked out into the blue, where the sea and the sky become one. A feeling of peace and understanding came over him. The pain in his side and the palpitations that he often felt in his heart had subsided to the point where his breathing was easier. The calmness of his body spread into his consciousness, and for a long time he gazed into the blueness that surrounded them.

Finally he walked over and stood near the captain. "It's real, all right. For me, it is. But no one sees the same thing in a rainbow, do they, Captain?"

Captain Biv placed a firm hand on the boy's shoulder. "'Tis true what ye say, lad. No one sees it the same, whether yer lookin' from within or from without. Count it as one o' God's miracles, a beautiful gift He colors the sky with, an amazin' display, and a sign to the soul of men."

"My dad told me there is wisdom in a rainbow. His father told him that he said there was a story, but he couldn't recall it. I wondered why he told me at all, if he couldn't remember." Theodore touched the steering wheel with his fingers and was not surprised when the captain stepped aside and gave the wheel to him.

"Sail 'er straight, lad," the captain commanded while he lit his pipe. "And I'll tell ye somethin' ye need to know."

"What's that?" Theodore asked.

"That yer dad is a wise man, fer what he done was to plant a seed that would grow in the fertile rows of yer imagination and bring ye here when yer heart and soul called fer it the most in yer life. He must've known ye needed more than a story to git past a stumblin' block. He knows ye that well."

Theodore looked beyond the bow of the schooner, where the sky blue of the sea grew deeper in color. Thoughts of his father and mother soothed his heart. He imagined their faces in the light mist that drifted on the breeze. He could hear their voices echoing as if they were far away. And Becky. The warmth of her hand was on his cheek. Her soft whisper at his ear. "Come back to me, Theo," she cried softly. The smell of her skin intoxicated the boy as he handed over the steering wheel to the captain and slowly moved away to a place at midship, where he laid down his head, resting it in the feathered softness of a pillow, and his body upon a warm pad of blankets.

"I'm with you, Theodore." Martha's thoughts entered his consciousness as he closed his eyes and felt the warmth of the Lab's body as she lay beside him. *"I will not leave you."* Her mind's voice was gentle as the breeze that urged the *Wind Sailor* on toward a sea

where color, rich and deep, would ply the boy's most inner thoughts.

"He's sleepin', Cap'n," Birdie assured Captain Biv while offering him a slice of his green apple.

The captain removed his pipe and plopped the tart chunk into his mouth. "It's best he rest now, fer soon we'll be comin' onto the mystical sea. His awakin' thar will be an eye opener, fer sure."

Both men smiled while the *Wind Sailor* cut quietly through the water toward the sea of wisdom.

The Indigo Sea

THE SEA BENEATH THE BLUE of the rainbow is called the Indigo. It is upon this sea that the energy of the Blue merges to a profound level. Lessons learned upon the other seas of the rainbow are here turned inward. A journey across this sea is a bridge between the finite and the infinite. It is here where the sailor's consciousness and spirit are revealed. Mystical boundaries are crossed, and enlightenment comes like bolts of lightning.

It was upon this sea that Theodore Clatterbuck finally opened his eyes to the excited barking of Martha, and the shouts from Birdie Wiggins. "Here they come, Cap'n!" Birdie yelled as he ran starboard toward the bow of the schooner. "I'm tellin' ye, I ain't never seen as many of 'em as this!" The little first mate made it to his place at the bow and cupped his hands above his brow. "Look at 'em, lad," he called. "Git up an' look at 'em!"

Theodore rubbed his eyes and stood up. Martha was standing on her hind legs, her front paws folded over the ship's gunnels. The boy moved quickly to her side and was immediately stunned at the sight before him.

The bright yet misty sky to the west was filled with fast-winged birds. They covered the sky like a windblown, ragged scarf, but they were beautiful in that they began maneuvering like rolling sea waves toward the schooner.

"What are they?" Theodore called to Birdie.

"Buntings," answered the first mate. "Indigo buntings. See how they're comin' like swells on the sea."

"But I thought that only mullpucks flew within the rainbow." Theodore had not seen any other birds than the mullpucks until now.

Birdie laughed out loud as he joined the boy and the Lab. "This is a lower sea, and often enough these finches will come in for a flight through color and to tempt the sea ladies from the depths.

"Sea ladies?" Theodore questioned.

"Yep. They're kinda like yer mermaids in the oceans of the earth, but they're faster in the water, smarter, and less tempting to a lost sailor's eyes. Their skin and scales is blue."

"You mean they are ugly?" Theodore asked while watching the buntings fly overhead.

"Well, they're not sirens, if that's what ye mean. But one named India, she's the queen of 'em, an' she's right fetchin', I must admit." Birdie pointed out to sea. "Watch them birds, now, and see how they're swoopin' down low. Their shadows is penetratin' the depths and excitin' the sea ladies, herdin' 'em up."

"But how do you know these creature are close by?" Theodore watched the gentle sea swells, hoping for a look at a sea lady.

"Them indigo buntings wouldn't be lingerin' here if they weren't. Watch now," he cautioned the boy.

"They'll come shootin' out the water soon to give them birds a show and some lessons in maneuverin'."

Soon after Birdie spoke, a sea lady burst through a shimmering swell, followed by two more, one on each side of her.

"That's India thar, in the front!" Birdie said in an excited voice. He pointed, "An' them two is her fastest sisters. The rest will be jumpin' in a second."

Theodore could hardly believe his eyes. "They're all the colors of the rainbow," he said. "And they have wings!"

"Yep. I fergot to tell ye that in all the excitement. Only India is indigo blue. The rest is the color of each sea in the rainbow. And yep, they kin fly! Perty, ain't they?"

By now, all of the sea ladies were leaping in unison out of the water and reentering the surf as if they were performing a choreographed show. An MGM water ballet could not have been staged better. Their swimming speed and ability to spring from the water and enter back in unison reminded Theodore of the porpoises he had seen doing the same thing on television shows.

It was funny to watch the play between the sea ladies and the divided flocks of finches that swooped down and cut sharp to the left and right. This went on for quite a while, until finally the buntings tired of the game and flew toward the sun.

Theodore watched them leave and then turned to Birdie. "Why did they stop?"

"They know instinctively how long they can stay in the rainbow realm."

"You mean there's a limit to how long one can remain here?" Theodore asked.

"Well, fer some it's longer than fer others."

"And what happens if birds stay longer then they should?"

Birdie scratched his nose and looked back at Captain Biv. The captain approached his first mate and Theodore.

"Then they stay forever," he offered.

"But how can that be?" Theodore wanted to understand. "I thought a rainbow was not a permanent vision. How can they stay forever? How long have you two been here?" Theodore looked at the captain and his first mate, waiting for an answer to a question he could not believe he had not already asked. "I mean, I thought a rainbow appears one minute and is gone the next. How is it that you and these sea ladies and everything from the pirates to the maiden of Rue Island and Spiley Rigor and his mullpucks can exist forever in something so fleeting as a rainbow?" Theodore watched the sea ladies follow India closer to the schooner. "Tell me that, Captain Biv," he said in a quiet challenge.

The captain looked at Birdie and then answered as precisely as he could, for in the Indigo Sea, a truth is felt beyond hearing. A truth spoken is inscribed within the soul of the one hearing it.

"Remember that a rainbow is a gift, lad. A beautiful vision ye kin call a miracle. Once seen, ye'll never fergit it, nor its magnificent colors. It's ingrained in yer memory so that even the mention of it conjures the vision. That alone keeps it alive. Me an' Birdie here, will always exist fer ye." The captain chuckled. "Even the ole rimcat will continue to guard the ledge of an island ye'll never fergit, 'cause it's in yer mind, now, lad. If all things are possible in the realm of a rainbow, then surely some dreams on earth from them who has been here kin certainly come true. But ye have to believe in what ye see. Don't leave the believin' here. Take it with ye when ye go."

Captain Biv looked over the side of the schooner. He waved and tipped his hat. "India," he said, "sea ladies." He placed his hand on Theodore's shoulder. "This here is Theodore Clatterbuck. He's a fine young man who has met the challenges of a voyage that began in the Red Sea. He is courageous and creative. He is humble and caring, wise and enthusiastic. His passion fer life, and his quest fer understandin' brought him here. He loves, and he's loved by them who know him and see him fer what he truly is. Kin he swim with ye, India?"

By now, the beautiful sea lady was lounging in the dark swells that lapped at the side of the schooner, surrounded by her colorful companions.

Theodore was mesmerized by her appearance. Never would he have imagined a creature such as she. But here she was, in plain sight and certainly as captivating as Birdie had said, with eyes the color of ripened blueberries and hair, radiant as the sun, with long, curly locks that seemed perfectly dry when raised from the water that glistened on her skin. Her nose was perfect, her chin, delicate, and on her lips, an intuitive smile formed that beckoned Theodore's trust.

"Hello, Theodore," India's voice was as gentle as the sun-streaked mist that is always light and drifting in the realm of the rainbow. She looked at Birdie and then at Captain Biv. "We raced the shadow of the buntings on our way here, Captain."

Captain Biv pulled his pipe from his mouth. "I figured ye'd be expectin' us," he noted. "This lad's been on a journey, India."

Martha barked, and the captain chuckled. "Oh, yes," he tussled the Lab's ears. "And Martha has been at his side the whole time."

Martha licked the captain's hand and looked back at India, satisfied.

"A swim through the Indigo Sea will bathe you in wisdom, Theodore," the sea lady began. "It will open your mind and spirit so that your awareness will be sharpened beyond your years. You will see life as it is and not as you once presumed it to be." She turned in the water and came closer to the schooner. "You must not be afraid to join us."

Theodore had never mastered the ability to swim. He had waded in the river below his house, and he could tread water. He could even hold his breath and dive in shallow water. But to enter the depths of the Indigo Sea and swim with sea ladies was a challenge that caused him to pause. "I'm not the best swimmer in the world," he admitted.

"You are in the realm of a rainbow now, Theodore," India assured him. "Anything is possible here, if you can imagine doing it."

Theodore swallowed and looked down at Martha. "What do you think, girl?" he asked nervously.

"I think you can do anything, Theodore," she thought. *"If you can imagine yourself swimming with these sea ladies, then I can see you doing it."*

Theodore knelt and put his arms around Martha's neck. He rubbed her face and patted her chest. "I'm going to do it, girl. I need to do this. Don't worry. I'll come back." Theodore looked at the Lab with tears in his eyes. "I want to come back. You know I do." Tears fell from the boy's eyes as he leaned his head against Martha's. She raised her paw and touched Theodore's knee. Then she licked his face.

"There is no doubt in my mind that you will return, and although I can't follow you in this, you must know that I am here for you."

Theodore stood up and wiped away his tears. His heart pounded in his chest as he climbed over the gunnel and sat with his legs dangling alongside the *Wind Sailor*. For a minute, he felt the pain in his side, and then he looked into the eyes of India and went past it in his mind. His entry into the water was not terrifying at all, for as soon as he entered, the sea ladies were there for him, supporting him.

"When you see past your fears, that is when your life truly begins," India spoke soothingly to the boy, her eyes not leaving his. "Now relax and come with us beneath the surface. Do not be afraid, Theodore, for as you allow the water to fill your lungs, you will be as you were at the beginning of your life in the womb of your mother."

Theodore placed his trust in the beautiful sea lady and then, turning his eyes up at Martha, he slipped beneath the surface of the Indigo Sea and into a world of lightness that was surreal yet familiar. The initial panic that he felt as the water began filling his lungs soon became overwhelming calmness. The air bubbles that blurred his vision during a brief struggle dissipated, and he was able to see clearly before him the calm and reassuring face of India. The other sea ladies swirled gracefully around him. Their thoughts were in his head just as Martha's were. The boy looked up and saw the captain and Birdie looking down at him. Martha barked her approval. *"Go, Theodore,"* her thought was clear in his mind. *"Go and swim with the sea ladies. I will be here awaiting your return."*

Theodore smiled as he reached up and waved his hand at the Lab. Then he turned toward India. "I am ready." The words formed in his mind were said with confidence.

The sea lady smiled. "Follow us, Theodore, and witness the freedom of your spirit." With that said, the sea lady turned in the water and placing her arms tightly along her sides, dove into the depths of the abyss. Theodore followed, his arms close to his sides, and was amazed at the speed at which he descended after her. He could sense the encouraging thoughts of the sea ladies as they fell deeper. *"Do not be afraid,"* India's thoughts were heard loud and clear, although he could plainly see her far ahead of him, her long, sleek body a silhouette now against a light that shown like prisms up from the depths of the sea. "*Fly!*" she commanded. At that instant, she and the sea ladies began moving through the water as if they were winged creatures moving as one, their underwater ballet performed against a backdrop of light and color such as the boy had never seen. The shadows they cast moved in and out of the light prisms so that it looked as if the ladies had multiple partners.

Theodore stopped in his descent and drifted there in the beauty of the moment. At times a sea lady would soar through the water so near him that he could feel the current of her passing. But he did not try to touch them. Instead, he floated there, weightless and mesmerized. He marveled at the great indigo curtains of water that surrounded him, and the light and shadows that played against them. He moved his hands and felt himself spinning, adrift in a great and silent space, where shards of light pricked painlessly at his skin and clothes. There was no pain in his body and gone were the palpitations of his heart that had frightened him all his life. There was no fear when India's voice came to him from where she swam far below.

"*Open your mind now, Theodore, and see the truth of your life.*" The sea lady's voice enticed the boy to look around him, for certainly a sign would appear from within the light or the shadows. But it was not until Theodore closed his eyes that he began to see the faces of those dearest to him. His mother and father, standing close by him. He could feel their hands upon his chest and forehead. Their voices in prayer and concern. His mother's tears fell into his heart and warmed his body. He could hear his father's whispers to God and the touch of a hand upon his chest. Voices came and went—caring voices, familiar ones. The sound of a door opening and closing. The warmth of Martha's body beside him. And then, a plea for forgiveness from one lost and confused. Theodore knew that voice. But it was another whose words beckoned him like no other to rise from his slumber, to fight for his life.

"Come back to me, Theodore," she said softly, her whisper tinged with emotion. A tear fell upon his lips, and he felt her kiss it away. "My heart is yours," she promised. "We have so much to do."

Becky. Theodore could feel himself struggling to rise. He tried to speak her name. *"I can hear you,"* he thought, wishing they could all hear him. *"I am here in the realm of the rainbow with India and the sea ladies. I've been on the Wind Sailor with Captain Biv and Birdie. Martha is here with me. I am safe but not finished with my journey."*

A sound like thunder rolled in the distance, and Theodore opened his eyes to the outstretched hand of India. *"Come,"* she beckoned. *"There is a storm looming."*

Theodore noticed that the deep indigo curtains of water were changing. *"What is happening?"* he projected, following the sea lady and her companions.

"We are entering another sea, Theodore. It is one that most humans cannot visualize at all. But it is important in your journey. Quick! There is not much time."

Theodore kept speed with the sea ladies and passed through red and blue currents into the last sea of the rainbow.

A View from the Violet Sea

THE VIOLET SEA OF THE RAINBOW is seen by few, for it is both a completion as well as a beginning of the energy vibration beyond the visible color spectrum. Its color variances extend from deep purple to pale lilac to bluish purple. These color variations are associated with high spiritual attainment, love for humanity and even sorrow. The Violet Sea can promote idealism and spark the imagination. It is a color of spiritual mystery. To view the world through the violet ray is to gain a knowledge of life which is difficult to attain in a single lifetime.

Perhaps it is for this reason that India saw purpose in bringing Theodore into the last sea of the rainbow.

"*Where is the Wind Sailor?*" Theodore wondered as he and the sea ladies sped through the water. "*Will it disappear with the rainbow? What about Martha?*" He wanted to know. "*Will she be all right?*"

"*Do not fret, Theodore.*" India understood the boy's concern. "*The Wind Sailor cannot be trapped within a rainbow or dissipate like a raindrop, for it is a vessel of hope and enlightenment that appears to those who dream it true. Believe me when I tell you that Martha is at your side even now.*"

Thunder rumbled as the sea ladies brought Theodore to the bottom of the sea, where light from the outer world shone through with a brilliance such that it was almost impossible for the boy to see.

"*Go, my sisters.*" Suddenly India turned and motioned for the sea ladies to go back into the darker waters. "*I will join you soon in the Indigo Sea of another rainbow. For this one is fading away.*"

One by one, the sea ladies swam past Theodore, each speaking his name and placing in his hand a colored stone. All except India did this.

"*You already possess the yellow stone from your visit to Clarity. These are possessions you can hold onto in the outer world. They are the physical proof of your journey.*"

Theodore looked at the beautiful stones in his hand and then began to stuff them into his pants' pocket before India suddenly stopped him.

"*No. Do not try to take them with you. Instead, push them through the bottom of the rainbow and let them fall to earth.*"

"*But they will be lost forever,*" the boy protested. "*And then no one will ever believe my story.*"

India smiled. "*They will not be lost, Theodore. And few will believe your story, anyway.*"

Theodore pulled the yellow stone from his pocket and added it to the others. "*Yes,*" he agreed. "*You're right about that, I guess.*" He seemed disappointed. "*They'll say I dreamed it all.*"

India understood. "*Perhaps they will. But in the realm of a rainbow, a dream is your reality. No one can take it away from you. For what you have experienced here will follow you the rest of your days on earth. Hold these lessons in your heart and always know that you are as special as you want to be. Set your goals and then follow them as you have here."*

Theodore smiled. He reached out his hand, and the sea lady touched it. *"I am ready to go home now,"* he thought.

India nodded her head. *"Go there."* She pointed down. *"And look at the earth through the violet ray. In your vision you will know the final lesson of the rainbow."*

Theodore swam past the sea lady.

"Goodbye, Theodore," he perceived her farewell. But when he looked back, she was gone.

Theodore did what India instructed and swam to the bottom of the sea to where, finally, he could see the earth below him. It was beautiful, with green trees and fields of grasses and flowers. He saw rivers and ponds and crops with workers attending them. He saw animals in their beds and people walking about in cities and towns, at the beaches and in the mountains. His vision was such that he could even see an ant climbing up the stem of a tomato plant. He saw his family and heard their voices in his mind. And then he heard the screech of brakes and Becky's scream. He saw the iron bridge and a boy hanging at the end of a rope. And he knew it was him. He could feel the pain around his waist and his heart pounding through his body. And the gasps of his breath. He watched as the old man lowered him to the ground and into Becky's arms.

"It's going to be all right, Theodore," she wept. "You stay with me." She rocked him in her arms. "Don't you go away," she pleaded. "Don't you leave me."

Then he heard a crash, and looking at the turn where the Iron Bridge Road forked, he saw the wreckage of Benny Jeter's truck and heard the moans and cries of the boys who had harmed him. In his heart, he was sorry for them, especially for the one he recognized as Bently Card. For in the twisted wreckage of his cousin's truck, the cruel boy cried out, broken and bleeding, to a God he had avoided all his life. A God Theodore was sure could hear the boy's cry. It was in that moment of Bently Card's pain and desperation, when Theodore was able to see into the life and saddened heart of his tormentor on earth. And what he saw brought such compassion to him that he knew beyond a shadow of a doubt what he must do. The final lesson of the rainbow was with him now. He could finally understand the joy in its mystery and the freedom in his journey to find it within himself.

Coming Home

THUNDER RUMBLED IN THE DISTANCE, and Theodore's eyes settled upon the face of a girl who stood at the edge of the yard behind his house. Her trembling lips moved, but he could not hear her words, for they were not intended for him. But the tears that glistened in her eyes spoke her heart's desire. He knew that.

Gently, Theodore pressed his fist through the bottom of the Violet Sea and opened his hand. He watched as the precious stones fell into the sky and disappeared. He then turned on his back and lay there, looking up through the fading colors of the rainbow seas.

"It is time to go home now." Words echoed in his mind. *Captain Biv, Birdie. Martha.*

Theodore closed his eyes for a moment, and when he opened them, he was back on the deck of the *Wind Sailor,* a full white sail that looked like a cloud was over his head. He sat up, and Martha greeted him anxiously with licks to his chin and neck. "Hey, girl," he said while trying to capture the face of the Lab in his hands. "I told you I'd come back." He hugged her and patted her shoulder, holding her close to him.

"We came out the rainbow jest as ye was 'bout to drop out the bottom of the sea, lad." Birdie's jolly voice brought Theodore to his feet.

"I guess that's a good thing," the boy replied while looking out over the thin, wispy clouds that surrounded them. He rose and walked to the portside of the schooner and looked down. "That's a long ways down."

Birdie laughed and patted the boy on the shoulder. "'Tis that, lad, fer sure. But we weren't 'bout to let ye fall out the bottom o' the sea, after all ye been through."

"Nope. Wouldn't let sech a thing happen to ye." Captain Biv approached the boy and leaned forward, his elbows on the gunnels of the vessel. "We're out o' the rainbow and headin' fer another formin' thar o'er yer house at the edge o' that big field."

Theodore looked past the bow of the schooner and recognized the field and the speck in the distance that was indeed his house. Then he looked again at the *Wind Sailor* and realized that it was the color of the sky, with sails like wispy clouds.

"I'm going home now," Theodore said. He knelt beside Martha. "I won't be able to hear your thoughts anymore, girl," he spoke softly. "But I'll never forget that you were here with me." He hugged the Lab.

"*Down there you don't need words to know what I think, Theodore,*" Martha thought her answer. "*I am here because there is no place I wouldn't follow you.*" Martha licked her human on his face. "*It's time to come home now, Theodore.*"

Theodore stood up, but now he was tired and hardly able to keep his eyes open. He walked back over to his pallet beneath the main mast and lay down. Martha followed him and nuzzled at his side.

Folding his hands over his chest, he took a deep breath and looked up into the faces of the captain and Birdie, who were standing over him. "I won't forget you, Captain Biv," he said through a faint smile. "And you, Birdie, and the *Wind Sailor.* We had some journey, didn't we?"

Captain Biv knelt down and touched the boy's hands. "That we did, lad. Ye come a long way and did well with it."

Birdie bent over and patted the boy on the shoulder. "And we'll not fergit ye, either, Theodore Clatterbuck. How could we ever?"

Theodore smiled and closed his eyes. The voices of the captain and Birdie became distant, as if they were leaving him while talking among themselves.

And soon the sound of the wind against the schooner's sails was all he could hear. That, and the breathing of Martha at his side.

"We'll take him home in that splash o' rainbow, thar, Birdie." Captain Roy G. Biv turned the *Wind Sailor* starboard. "Lower them sails a bit, mate, and we'll come about on a shall'a sea fer the lad's return."

"Aye, Cap'n." Birdie lowered the mainsail, walked to the bow of the schooner and looked over into the yard of the Clatterbuck's house. "She's a perty little thing, fer sure, awaitin' the lad, Cap'n."

Captain Biv chuckled. "He's one what's worth the wait, Birdie."

The first mate nodded his head in agreement as the *Wind Sailor* came upon the shallow waters of the rainbow. "It's a pale one here, Cap'n, but thar's thunder to the west."

"We'll surely sail fer it, Birdie!" the captain answered. "But first, thar's a family and a perty little lass what needs their boy back." Captain Biv left his place at the helm and walked over to where Theodore lay sleeping.

"Wake now, lad," he said while gently pressing on Theodore's hands. "Yer home again."

WHEN BECKY OPENED HER EYES after her prayer, she was amazed at what she saw around her. The scent of the recent afternoon rain shower that had drenched the ground was still in the air, and there was rumbling in the western sky. But there at the Clatterbuck's little house at the edge of the field was a rainbow. She was in awe as she walked around the yard, noticing that the colorful arch had formed over the house. Its colors, though brilliant, bathed the air around the house in misty hues that rendered the area mystical.

"God," the girl said beneath her breath as she stood there in wonder.

"Becky!" Bea Clatterbuck called excitedly from the kitchen door that led out onto a screened-in porch at the rear of the house. "Becky, come quick!" The woman was breathless as she flung open the screen door. "He's awake!"

After a brief hospital stay, Virgil and Bea had brought their son home. Doctors had assured them that although there was trauma to Theodore's body from the incident at the iron bridge, there had been no broken bones, and his heart seemed stronger than ever. There was severe bruising to his midsection, and one side in particular seemed to cause him much discomfort. But all said, he would mend well. There was some concern as to why he had not fully awakened during the period, as there was nothing to explain his almost constant sleep state. The few times that he had opened his eyes, he seemed unable to focus, and any response to the coaxing of his parents or Becky was met at best with incoherent mumbles from the boy.

His doctor felt that the trauma inflicted upon him both physically and mentally had taken such a toll that he would have to sleep his way through it, and the familiarity of home was a better place than in the hospital.

"The body is healing itself," the doctor had told them. "And perhaps, so is his mind." Dr. Wilbur Anthony truly believed this to be the case, and he strived to reassure the family that Theodore would certainly wake up and be fine. "We must give him time," the doctor advised when he came by the house the next day to look in on the boy and take his vital signs. "He's looking good. Much better than the boys who did this to him."

"They deserve the pain," Bea had told the doctor. But not without a feeling of guilt. She was not a vengeful person, but the lengths the boys had gone to in harming her son tinged her with anger. *How could anyone be so cruel?* She had wondered. *And why my son? A boy who had never harmed anyone in his life.*

"There is no way to truly understand what makes a person a bully," Dr. Anthony explained while sitting in a chair beside Theodore's bed. "You would have to live with them and see their lives. You would have to look into their hearts and find the source of the sadness and anger that drives them. Once in a while it's obvious, but most times not. The best thing is most bullies learn a lesson and grow out of it. The ones who don't live pretty pathetic lives."

"But what about the victims?" Virgil had asked. "What about our son and what he has to endure?"

There was much emotion in the man's voice as he had posed his questions to the doctor.

Dr. Anthony pursed his lips and shook his head slowly. "Some of them suffer it. Others stand up to it. Usually that will stop it, but not always. The mental scars can last a lifetime. And then there are those who somehow find it in themselves to deal with it and put it in its place." The doctor had then looked into the faces of Virgil and Bea Clatterbuck and added, "I'm not sure where Theodore stands in all of this. But he's a good young man. Smart as a whip from what everybody says. And I'll wager that he comes through it all right."

Bea had fought back her tears that day. "I didn't mean to be heartless, Dr. Anthony. But I have to wonder if those boys will wear the scars they received in that accident as reminders of what they did."

"I would think so, Bea," answered the doctor. "Benny Jeter lost his truck and will smart from a toothless grin until his folks can afford a good set of dentures for him. Blue Daniel's broken arm and leg will keep him out of baseball for a while, and Jerry Rust will carry that gash in his lip for the rest of his life."

"And what about Bently Card?" Bea had asked. "He's the worst one of all."

The doctor grimaced as he pondered the woman's question. He stood up and closed his medical bag as he was about to leave. "Well, Bea, Virgil..." He had looked at the couple and then back at their son lying on the bed. "Well, he's in the worst shape of all `of them and broken up pretty bad. He's going to have a lot of time to think about what he has done. How that will end up, I'm not sure." The doctor left just minutes before Theodore woke up.

WHEN BECKY ENTERED THE BEDROOM, Theodore smiled at her.

"Hi, Becky," he said. "Where have you been?"

The girl crossed the room and stood at Theodore's bedside, her arms folded in front of her. Tears welled in her eyes as she answered. "I've been standing in a rainbow and praying you would come back to me." A tear coursed down her cheek as she bent down and kissed the boy she loved.

Martha, whose head was resting on Theodore's folded hands, repositioned herself between the girl and boy and hunkered down low and close to her human's side in the bed. The Lab was much more willing to share him than to give up her place beside him.

Becky smiled and wiped the tears from her eyes. She walked to the other side of the bed and sat on its edge.

Theodore opened his hand, and she laced her fingers with his.

"Um," the boy responded. "Praying in a rainbow is bound to get you something."

Becky smiled and squeezed his hand. "And how about you. Where have you been?"

Theodore looked at the girl and then at his mother and father standing at the foot of his bed. He touched Martha on the head and found her eyes searching his. "Well, that's a long story that will have to wait."

The Lab snuggled at Theodore's side and closed her eyes.

"Now, tell me." Theodore put one hand behind his head. "What has been going on while I was away?"

Bea and Virgil Clatterbuck did not leave their son's room that night until long after midnight. Becky stayed as long as she could. Calls were made, and Dr. Anthony returned and pronounced Theodore fit as a fiddle and ready to rest a lot and ease himself back into action.

Mr. Lynn came by to visit the next day and brought Miss Durkmeyer. Mayor Bloom and his wife brought Becky over the day after that and stayed for supper, which they brought with them. Mr. Horton checked in on the boy daily. Benny Jeter's father came by and expressed his disappointment that his son had participated in such a thing. Benny showed up the next day and apologized. He brought Blue with him. The boy said he was ashamed. Jerry Rust's family had sent their son away to work on an uncle's farm for the summer.

Slowly Theodore regained his strength until one July day while he was sitting in the grass of his back yard, he heard Becky's voice as she rounded the corner of the house on her bike. She dropped the bike in the grass and hurried over to where Theodore was sitting. "You are never going to believe what I've found in the river on the way over here," she said, reaching deep into the oversized pocket of her khaki trail pants. "I looked over the bridge rails and saw them in the still water next to the rock where we launched our raft last summer." The girl withdrew her hand from her pocket and held it closed in front of Theodore's face. "Are you ready?" she asked.

"Ready," Theodore answered.

"Look at these." Becky opened her hand and spread the contents over her palm. "Have you ever seen stones so beautiful?" she asked, touching each one with her fingers. "They were just lying there, as if someone had dropped them from out of the sky. There are seven of them." The girl counted them and placed them in Theodore's hand. "Where do you think they came from?" she asked.

Martha, who was sitting close by the boy, sniffed the stones and licked his hand. Then she sat as if waiting for an answer she already knew.

Theodore picked up each stone and rolled them between his forefinger and thumb. "These are mine," he answered, "All except one," he put aside the yellow stone, "were given to me by the sea ladies in the Violet Sea."

Becky was quiet as she listened. When Theodore

did not continue, she touched the yellow stone. "And what about this one, Theo, where did this one come from?"

Theodore did not hesitate to answer the girl, for there was no one in the world he trusted more.

"I picked it up from a pathway I walked along in a city named Clarity." He looked up from the stones and into Becky's eyes. "I've been through a rainbow, Becky, and I want to tell you what I found. Can you listen to my story and try to believe it?" Tears welled in the boy's eyes as he opened his heart to the girl.

Becky put her hand to her mouth as if she were recalling a lost memory. For some moments she did not answer. And then she lowered her hand and moved closer to Theodore. "On that day at the iron bridge," she talked slowly, "there was a shower and thunder nearby. Just a few droplets on my shoulders as I held you there in my arms. And when I looked up into the sky, I prayed to God for a sign that you would be okay. Tears clouded my eyes, and I couldn't see," Becky's voice was choked with emotion, but she continued. "And then, through the tears, I saw the colors of a rainbow, and I knew that you would come back to me. It was like a promise from God. And I believed it. Later, I opened my eyes from a prayer here in your yard and found the whole place surrounded by a rainbow. It was then that your mother came out of the house with the news that you were awake." Becky wiped tears from her eyes and breathed deeply. Then she leaned toward the boy and said, "You left in a rainbow and came back through one. Now tell me your story, Theodore Clatterbuck, and I will believe you. Why shouldn't I?"

Two hearts were open that July afternoon, and a story was told of a journey like no other.

BENTLY CARD LOOKED UP from his food tray on the patio of his parents' house, where he had spent most of his summer days alone. The weeks since the accident had done little to improve his physical condition. His pain was constant, but he tried to ignore it, telling himself that it could have been worse. His broken legs would mend well enough for him to walk again. But that was all he could expect from them. His participation in sports was over. Screws and metal rods, not to mention a silicon ball joint, were just not conducive with being the fleetest of athletes. *A waste. A stupid waste.* He thought that often enough. But it was his own doing. Benny was not to blame. Neither was Blue nor Jerry. And certainly not the boy who was now standing in front of him.

Bently lowered his eyes in shame. After a moment, he tried looking at the boy, but it was hard. Instead, he looked away and spoke, "Okay, Clatterbuck, what do you want?" Bently's question was an attempt at the abrasiveness he had always been so good at. "What? Do you want to see the sentence for my sin? Well, here it is," he pushed the tray away, sending it crashing onto the slate patio. "How do you like it, huh? Broken up legs. Can't walk. Probably will have to limp for the rest of my life, and why? Because I..." Bently could not finish his tirade. It was too hard. He just stopped and hung his head for a minute before he looked up again. "What do you want from me, Clatterbuck?" he asked, almost pleadingly. "You want me to say I'm sorry?" There was resentment in his voice.

Theodore walked over and picked up the food tray.

"Don't do that," Bently protested in a quiet voice.

Theodore reset the legs of the tray and placed it back in front of Bently. He picked up the broken pieces of a porcelain plate and laid them in a pile on the tray. Then he placed the plastic cup Bently had been drinking from into its basket in the corner of the tray.

"Are you?" Finally Theodore spoke. "Are you really sorry?" he posed his question differently this time. "Because, if you are, then that is great for you." He walked over to a chair and sat down, his wrists resting on his knees. "But even if you are sorry for what you did, it doesn't change anything. Your legs are still broken, and I'm still who I am. But if you are sorry, and I accept that, then it is a start. Not just for you but for me, also. And it would be good for us both."

"Yeah? How's that, Clatterbuck? Tell me how this works." Bently's effort at coolness failed, and although his words were phrased to belittle, the venom behind them had weakened.

Theodore continued, "Well, I don't think you're

going to be a track star anytime soon, or even ever from this point on. So that brings you down to about my speed, which will make it easier for us to hang out some, if you want to. I know a lot of great places to hike to and some fun things to do that won't get you locked up one day." Theodore stood up and walked over to Bently. "So, if you want to apologize, and you really mean it, then fine, I'll accept. But even if you don't, you need to know that you're off the hook with me, anyway."

"How's that?" Bently was trying to make sense of this. No one he had ever taunted or hurt had invited him to hang out with them. And Theodore Clatterbuck was the last person he would have expected a show of friendship from.

"Here it is, Bently." Theodore looked the boy straight in the eyes and without blinking said, "I forgive you for what you did to me at the iron bridge and for all the other awful things you've done and said to me. You are free, and I mean that." Theodore extended his hand and waited until Bently reached out and gripped it.

"Thanks," the boy said.

Theodore smiled and turned to walk away.

"I am, you know," Bently cleared his voice. "I am sorry."

Theodore smiled and nodded. "I'll be around, if you want to get together sometime." He turned to leave.

"Maybe when school starts up, Clatterbuck," Bently spoke up. "They say I should be walking better by then."

"Call me, Theo." Theodore smiled and left.

Theodore felt good that day as he left the home of his former nemesis. For on that day, he realized that forgiveness was the greatest gift he brought back from his journey through a rainbow. And that, alone, brought freedom and clarity to his soul.

The End

TITLES BY FRANCIS EUGENE WOOD

The Wooden Bell (A Christmas Story)
The Legend of Chadega and the Weeping Tree
Wind Dancer's Flute
The Crystal Rose
The Angel Carver
The Fodder Milo Stories
The Nipkins (Trilogy)
Snowflake (A Christmas Story)
The SnowPeople
Return to Winterville
Winterville Forever
Autumn's Reunion (A Story of Thanksgiving)
The Teardrop Fiddle
Two Tales and a Pipe Dream
The Christmas Letter
Tackle Box Memories
Moonglow
Sunflower
The Keeper of the Tree
The Toy Maker's Son
The Enchantment of Nebulon Grey
Journey Through a Rainbow
Tackle Box Memories Vol. 2

These books are available through the author's
Website: www.tipofthemoon.com
Email address: fewwords@moonstar.com

Write to:
Tip-of-the-Moon Publishing Company
175 Crescent Road
Farmville, Virginia 23901

The author and his chocolate Lab, Coco.

FRANCIS EUGENE WOOD is an award-winning Virginia author whose stories have entertained readers both young and old since the release of his first book, *The Wooden Bell (A Christmas Story),* in 1996. *Journey Through a Rainbow* is his twenty-fourth book. Francis writes from his home in Buckingham County, Virginia.

CPSIA information can be obtained at www.ICGtesting.com
Printed in the USA
BVOW07s1442260713

326545BV00004B/9/P